Where Sleeping Dragons Lie

DRAGON SHIFTERS OF ELYSIA BOOK ONE

CRISTINA RAYNE

Fantastical Press

ALSO BY CRISTINA RAYNE

Riverford Shifters

Tempted by the Jaguar

Accepting the Jaguar

Rescued? by the Wolf

Tempted by the Tiger

Tempted by the—Lion?

Suspecting the Lioness *coming soon

Elven King Series

Shadows Beneath the Falling Snow (A Prequel Story)

Claimed by the Elven King

Date Night: A Bonus Short

Claimed by the Elven Brothers

The Elven Realms

(Sequel series to the Elven King series)

Memories of an Elven Prince

To Love an Elven Prince *coming Summer 2021

Dragon Shifters of Elysia

Where Sleeping Dragons Lie

When Fire Dragons Fall

What Stubborn Dragons Want

What Fire Dragons Treasure

Lords of the Vampire Underground

Tales from the Vampire Underground Collection

A Whisper in the Darkness *coming soon

Incarnations of Myth

Seeking the Oni

Falling for Enma *coming soon

Fractured Multiverse

(Writing as C.G. Garcia)

The Supreme Moment: Kairos

The Supreme Moment: Externus *coming soon

Black Crimson *coming soon

The Golden Mage Trilogy

The Kingdom of Eternal Sorrow

The Man Within the Temple

The Last Stone Cast

To my readers who are always excited for the next paranormal romantic journey

"You know, you're practically drooling, right?" Briana said with amusement as she watched her friend, Carol, stare down with bright, excited eyes at the book she had brought from her late grandmother's collection as though the book was the true *Book of the Dead*.

"If there weren't customers milling about, I would be squealing like a little girl seeing a unicorn in her backyard," Carol joked.

"From your reaction, I take it Granny Ruth never showed this book to you, either?"

Some of the excitement dimmed from the older woman's eyes. "No. She must've acquired it right before she—passed. Or rather, I imagine it was a sudden, unexpected find given that she never mentioned that she was hunting for anything even remotely like this beauty."

Briana's eyes once again fell on the old, leather-bound book that Carol was carefully examining with gloved hands. The leather appeared to have darkened over the years, whether naturally or because of the preservation efforts of its previous owners remained to be seen. There were a few cracks along the spine from years of being open and read, though there was thankfully no initial evidence of red rot.

"The book was on the center shelf in her rare books case," Briana said. "I must've walked by it dozens of times over the past month before I finally noticed it."

"Maybe because of the archival sleeve?" Carol offered absently as she carefully opened the book to its title page. "It's the same type Ruth used for all her rare books, so I wouldn't think it would particularly catch your eye." She raised her eyes and looked back at Briana with a flash of grief. "Plus, you've had too many things weighing on your mind and heart these days to notice something as innocuous as a new book."

Briana shook her head. "But I *shouldn't* have had to notice it at all. Granny Ruth *always* called me the moment she found a book even remotely interesting, but an obvious treasure like *this*? You haven't said much about it, but all teasing aside about the drooling, I can see it in your eyes. This book is something special. Even factoring in her heart attack—" She cut herself off, a knot of grief abruptly forming in her throat before she forced it down and shook her head again. "It's just—strange," she continued thickly.

"Hmm...it doesn't appear to have been oiled by its previous owners. I don't see even a hint of bleed-through along the spine." Carol suddenly gasped, and her eyes narrowed. "What—*is* this?"

"I know, right?" Briana replied with an excited grin, reaching down with a white-gloved hand to point at a series of strange, fading symbols that were handwritten —or drawn—on what she assumed was the title page. "I figured this was why there wasn't any kind of title etched into the spine. The writing doesn't even remotely match any kind of alphabet I've ever seen. The whole book is written in it. I might be jumping the gun here, but it reminds me a lot of the *Voynich* manuscript, only without the strange pictures."

Carol looked over at her sharply before carefully opening the book a few pages in. "Don't tease me like that. I don't recognize the writing either, but for all we know, this could just be a prank or someone's old journal written in their own personal cipher."

Briana nodded. "I thought so, too. I didn't want to get you excited for nothing, so I took a few pictures with my phone of blocks of writing from different pages and ran them through an online image search. The search brought up a lot of pictures of old vellum, handwritten pages, but none of the writing on them even remotely matched these—letters?"

"I can see why you would hesitate to call them that," Carol said. "Each line of writing just looks like a stretched out water hose twisted with kinks here and there of various-sized loops surrounded by a random number of dots and diagonal, short lines. The writing in the *Voynich* manuscript at least had letters that *resembled* our alphabet."

"A water hose, huh," Briana echoed with a grin. "I was thinking more along the lines of a weirdly embellished EEG line, but a twisted up water hose works, too."

The older woman snorted. "You would have water hoses on the brain, too, if you had spent a couple of hours spraying weed killer onto your lawn this morning like I had, but go ahead and laugh at an old woman."

"I wouldn't dream of it. Don't bite the hand that feeds you and all that."

A familiar bell abruptly chimed behind her, signaling that a customer had entered the bookshop.

"Oh, shoot," Carol muttered as she began to take her gloves off. "I forgot I had an appointment this morning.

A new client." Her eyes flitted longingly back down to the book they had been examining.

"I'm not going anywhere," Briana assured her. "I don't have any more lectures today, so we can study the book together all day if *you* can spare the time."

Carol still looked torn. "If he weren't so interested in buying my latest acquisition, I would reschedule and close up shop for the rest of the day, but…"

"Go," Briana said, giving her back a nudge towards the door. "I'll call Melody in the meantime and see how soon she can fit us in to have the book carbon dated."

"Good idea."

Ten minutes later, Briana was just ending her call with Melody when the door suddenly opened to reveal Carol. Surprised, Briana opened her mouth to ask if the older woman had forgotten something before the words froze in her throat when she realized that someone was following Carol into the room.

A black-haired man dressed in a stylish, black suit sans tie that wouldn't have looked out of place at a celebrity red carpet event paused behind her friend just a couple of steps beyond the threshold. His age could have been anywhere from late twenties to mid-thirties. His short hair was just a bit longer in front and artfully tousled, and he had about a couple of days' worth of stubble above his upper lip and along his jawline.

This was Carol's new client?

He turned his head slightly from left to right as he briefly glanced around the room until his gaze abruptly paused, then settled on her, his expression openly curious.

He was so far afield from the shop's usual clientele that Briana was thoroughly caught off guard, and it took every ounce of her self-control to keep her expression neutrally friendly when confronted so abruptly by the face of one of the most gorgeous men she had seen in possibly *ever*.

"This is Mr. Taron Hildebrand. Excuse us for a moment," Carol told her absently as she led the striking man to the series of glass cases that took up the entire back wall of the shop's examining room.

The older woman paused in front of a case that contained the rarest books in the shop's collection. Briana's heart sped up in a different kind of excitement. The store's finances had been getting worryingly lean this year no matter how hard Carol had been trying to hide that fact from her, and one big sale could instantly turn that all around.

Carol was Granny Ruth's best friend, and over the years of spending countless hours researching and obsessing over the ancient tomes that came in and out of this rare books shop with the two older women, she had become much the same to Briana. Had she not had Carol to lean on and mourn with, Granny Ruth's abrupt death would have destroyed her. Her friend deserved this windfall and more.

"I apologize for making you come back here," Carol said, her voice breaking through Briana's dark thoughts. "I had a bit of unexpected excitement this morning and didn't get to transfer the book to one of the viewing cases in my office."

"It's fine," Mr. Hildebrand assured her in a strong, totally sexy and British-accented bass that seemed to reverberate throughout the room and pleasantly over her senses. "I had hoped for an opportunity to physically examine the book during this meeting."

With an internal sigh, Briana carefully closed her grandmother's mysterious book. It seemed her continuing examination of the book would have to wait, at the very least another hour, until Carol was finished with her appointment.

"I'll give you two some privacy." She carefully picked up the book. "Carol, I'll just put this in an empty case in your office while I go out for breakfast in the meantime."

Briana focused her attention on Carol's gorgeous new client just as he was turned to look back at her over his shoulder. "Can I offer you some tea, coffee, or juice, Mr. Hilde—"

Her words cut off in a sharp gasp as his eyes had fallen on the leather book in her still-gloved hands and in the next second, all but lunged towards her with a wild, scary look in his eyes. She instinctually flinched away and took a couple of unconscious steps back until the small of her back bumped into the examining table's edge.

As her mind shrieked in warning, Mr. Hildebrand stopped just short of touching distance and then all her frantic mind could focus on was a pair of strangely orange-tinted hazel eyes the color of an ocean sunset regarding her with an intense, laser focus, even while her heart was threatening to beat out of her chest.

"I'll pay you five hundred thousand dollars for that book right now without examination," he offered firmly, both hands raised slightly towards her with fingers flexing as though he longed to just snatch the book away from her.

Briana swallowed against the knot of fear that had suddenly formed in her throat and exchanged a quick, startled look with Carol, whose frozen, shocked expression probably mirrored her own.

"I'm sorry," she replied slowly, struggling not to

squirm under that fierce, unnerving gaze, "but this one isn't currently for sale."

After a horribly tense, though brief, moment of silence where even the very air seemed to be holding its breath, the corners of his lips slowly quirked up into a mild grin while those sunset eyes continued to bore into her disconcertingly. "I figured as much, but I had to offer all the same."

He took a few steps back until she no longer felt as though her personal space was being invaded, and his expression turned sheepish as he joined his hands together behind his back into a more relaxed pose. "I thought I recognized—well, forgive me. It seems my enthusiasm got the best of me again, and I gave you an unintentional shock. That was terribly rude of me."

Gripping her grandmother's book a bit more tightly, Briana straightened and offered him a small smile of forgiveness even though all her senses were still screaming *danger*! "That someone can get that excited about a book in this day and age should make us all happy."

He chuckled. "Indeed." He looked over his shoulder and nodded towards Carol, who was currently watching their exchange with anxious eyes, before turning back to Briana. "Perhaps I'll have better luck with the volume I initially came to examine. If it's not too much trouble, I'll accept a cup of black tea with a dash of cold milk if you have it—or if not, a cup of coffee, black, will be fine."

Despite some lingering misgivings about leaving her friend alone with Mr. Hildebrand, Briana nodded. "I'll be just a minute."

Carol's bookshop had a small coffee and cappuccino bar in the front to cater to both the casual browser fresh off the street and the serious rare book collectors that had become regular buyers over the years. As she waited for Carol's part-timer, Misty, to prepare a cup of black tea to order, Briana's pulse still continued to race even though it was several minutes after that initial shock.

In that split-second when Taron Hildebrand had shot towards her, she imagined that sudden burst of terror she had experienced was the same terror a rabbit felt in the face of an unexpected viper's strike. Maybe that's why her heart still couldn't be calmed. His alarming behavior, on top of being observed with such uncanny eyes, had triggered all the warning bells in her mind. Was she a complete idiot to ignore them for the sake of being polite to a new client and a desperately needed lucrative sale?

The sound of a door creaking open had her neck instantly craning towards the back of the shop. Although she shouldn't have been, Briana was still surprised to see Mr. Hildebrand hurrying back into the sales room with an anxious-looking Carol a few steps behind. His cell phone was pressed against his left ear, drawing her eyes to the slight frown and intense expression darkening his eyes. He gave her a curt, distracted nod as he passed the coffee counter on his way to the shop's exit.

The clanging of the bells on the entrance door was still echoing in the shop as Briana turned to Carol with a bewildered look. "What happened?"

Carol sighed. "Just plain old rotten luck, I would guess. I had just placed the book he came to examine on the table when he suddenly received a phone call. I could tell he was irritated with the interruption, the way the muscles in his face kind of hardened, but he answered it immediately, nonetheless."

"Something work related?" Briana hazarded.

"Probably. He hung up rather quickly and apologized for having to cut his appointment short. Then he headed towards the door, telling me over his shoulder he'd call and reschedule."

"Tea?" Misty offered with a wry grin, setting the steaming cup of black tea she had been preparing for their wayward guest in front of Briana.

"Sure." She picked up the teacup and gestured towards the back with her free hand. "I hate that your potential buyer flaked out on us, but I'm really dying to get back to examining Granny Ruth's book. Breakfast can wait. Do you think Joseph would be willing to drive up to meet with us tomorrow morning? If anyone has a chance of knowing anything about that strange writing, it would be him."

Carol snorted. "That man would drive through a tornado blocking the road if he knew a prize such as that intriguing book awaited him on the other side."

"Stupid question, right," Briana said with a grin. "Speaking of, Mr. Hildebrand seemed just as passionate. I can't believe he's never come sniffing around here or some of the local auction houses before today. Did he just move into the area, or was he referred by one of the regulars? That's not the kind of man that I would forget seeing, especially in our circles."

"Yes, he certainly was handsome," Carol replied with a chuckle. "Terrance referred him, said he was from New York City. I suppose he ran into Mr. Hildebrand during his last trip to the East Coast, but I don't know for sure. You know Terrance. He can talk about a book without interruption for days, but when it comes to everything else, he's always short on details."

"Well, if he came all this way just to buy one of your books, then I think we'll be seeing him pretty soon, hopefully after Joseph examines Granny's mystery book." Briana shook her head as she stepped into Carol's office to retrieve the book in question. "Offering us five hundred grand after a single glimpse—that's just crazy."

"Or calculating. I could swear that he actually recognized it."

Briana frowned. "With no writing anywhere on the exterior? It looks like a thousand other old, hand-bound leather books. I never would've given it a second glance if I didn't know Granny's cases like the back of my hand and realized it didn't belong."

"You'd be surprised."

"I had planned on leaving it here overnight, but maybe I should take it with me back home after all. Although he was drool-worthy, Mr. Hildebrand gave off some really strange vibes. I mean, my heart nearly tore out of my chest when he came at me so suddenly."

Looking troubled, Carol slowly nodded. "I didn't want to say—I thought it was just me, but—yes, I think that would be best."

CHAPTER TWO

"Carol! You won't *believe* what I just found in the —" Briana called out excitedly as she pushed open the bookshop door to the sound of bells before stopping mid-phrase when she realized that her friend had visitors.

At the sound of her voice, the two men standing at the reception counter in the center of the shop, one gray-haired and dressed in a standard gray business suit and the taller, black-haired one in a more casual charcoal-colored sport coat and black slacks, turned to look over at her. Briana instantly froze a step inside the shop, her hand still clenched around the brass doorknob and the other contracting tightly around the strap of her oversized shoulder bag. She stared mutely at the taller man, at Taron Hildebrand, who regarded her with an opaque expression in his eyes.

"I'm—sorry," Briana forced out past the huge knot of surprise that had instantly formed in her throat. "I didn't realize you were with clients."

Her pulse began to race when Mr. Hildebrand turned around completely and started to walk towards her, a smile forming on his full lips. "Just the person I was hoping to meet with this morning." He reached out a hand. "Once again, my name is Taron Hildebrand."

Willing herself not to show just how flustered she was feeling, Briana released the stranglehold she had on her shoulder bag's strap and accepted his hand for a shake with a professional smile. "Briana Wright. It's nice to meet you, Mr. Hildebrand."

"Just 'Taron' is fine."

Flashing her another smile, he stepped back a few paces, allowing her to step more fully into the shop and close the door. "Briana, as in the character from *The Faerie Queene?*"

"Only the spelling, thank goodness," she replied with a shrug. "Briana was such a shallow, terrible character. My mother wasn't into reading the classics."

Although she could guess exactly why he wanted to meet with her, Briana decided not to humor him, client or no client. Especially not when she was dying to tell

Carol—and later Joseph—about what she had discovered in the book just this morning.

"You said you wanted to meet with me," she continued before he could even open his mouth to speak. "I'm sorry for the misunderstanding, but I'm not an employee here. Like you, I'm just a patron and friend of the shop owner."

Those uncanny, sunset eyes bored into her without blinking. "Yes, but the book I saw you examining yesterday *is* owned by you, correct?" Taron said.

"It's still not for sale, no matter how much you offer me," Briana countered quickly, putting a bit of apology in her tone.

"It's slightly more complicated than that, I'm afraid," he said, the intensity of his stare not waning a bit, making her want to squirm in discomfort.

"Mr. Hildebrand believes the book is an old family heirloom his family has been searching for since it went missing in the early nineteenth century," Carol sudden spoke up, making Briana jump.

She had completely forgotten her friend and the older, unknown man that had likely accompanied Hildebrand were also in the shop while she and this intimidating man talked. "An heirloom?" she echoed incredulously.

Taron nodded eagerly. "Although I would have to

examine it more meticulously to be sure, the blackened color of the leather on the book's upper, right-hand corner suggesting that it had once been singed, as well as the absence of any writing or etchings on the outside cover, even along the spine, fits the description my ancestors left of it in diaries and letters. Also, to a lesser extent, an image of a book just as I've described makes an appearance in a few family paintings that have been passed down through the generations. I, of course, have brought photos of both the letters and the paintings." He gestured towards the silent stranger at the counter. "I've also brought along an appraiser I have worked with for many years while living in New York."

Briana felt her heart once again speed up, but this time in rising excitement instead of trepidation. Could she possibly be on the brink of solving the book's mystery so early in the game? Did she dare hope?

The appraiser approached them and offered her his hand. "Harold Brown. I am the owner of the Brown Auction House in New York City and an expert in rare books and ancient documents."

She gave his hand a firm shake. "It's nice to meet you, too."

"Perhaps everyone would like to continue this conversation in the privacy of my office?" Carol offered, looking questionably at Briana rather than the two men.

Not wanting to give away her mounting excitement, Briana focused her attention on Taron and said with a touch of hesitation, "Before I agree to allow you to examine my book Mr.—excuse me—*Taron,* may I ask you a couple of questions about your heirloom book?"

His gaze sharpened. "Ask me anything."

"Describe its interior—was a printing press used or was it handwritten? What language did the author use, and were there any illustrations included?"

He grinned slowly, and suddenly a shudder of unease inundated her body as this new expression made her inexplicably feel as though he was presenting her with a show of weapons rather than something as benign as a smile. What the hell was wrong with her? Or *him?*

Yes, his eyes were a little bit creepy, and he was gorgeous enough to fluster her. Yet, other than startling her yesterday with his sheer excitement over Granny Ruth's book, he had really done nothing that explained why being in his presence, alone, put her so much on edge.

Maybe she should've declined his request for a meeting from the get-go and waited for Joseph to arrive, after all...

"Oh, it was very much handwritten—given that it was written using an alphabet I really doubt more than a handful of people have seen over the ages, much less know how to read," Taron answered. "As for illustrations, there was only one, located about a third of the book in and drawn by someone with what were probably only rudimentary artistic skills. A key."

Briana could feel the heat of her excitement rise in her cheeks as Taron held out his hand to his appraiser. His description was a bit too on the nose for her to discount. She watched with curiosity and an eagerness she could no longer hide as Mr. Brown opened up the leather briefcase he was carrying and pulled out a set of 4x6 photos which he handed to Taron.

He quickly shuffled through them before selecting one and then holding it out to her. "This key."

The picture was of what looked like a charcoal sketch of a double-bitted key with a dragon head on a yellowing piece of stained canvas. A tiny gasp escaped her lips. It looked remarkably similar to the very drawing she had discovered in the book only this morning, down to the shape of the two teeth and the style of the horned-dragon head that made up the key's head. That picture was the reason she had rushed over to the bookshop at the crack of dawn today.

Before she could comment, Taron handed her two more photos. The first shot was a small oil painting of a close-up of four dark-haired women with similar features and of varying ages. They stood in a parlor room, the youngest handing a *very* familiar-looking leather-bound book with a darkened corner on the front cover to the oldest of the other three.

The second photo was a portrait of a different woman in a different style of dress that was sitting before a fireplace in a room lit only by the oil lamp on a small table next to her chair. On the table next to the lamp was the same leather-bound book, blank spine facing the viewer.

"Okay, you definitely piqued my interest," Briana admitted with a small smile.

"Briana, go ahead and escort these gentlemen to my office. I'll prepare some tea for our guests."

The thought of being alone with Taron Hildebrand without Carol acting as a buffer didn't really sit well with her, but she nodded anyway. What was a little discomfort when there were some answers to be had?

"If it's all right with you, Carol," Briana said, "we can skip the office discussion and go straight back to the examining room." She patted the side of her shoulder bag, drawing the two men's eyes to it. "I already have the book in question here."

Taron looked as though he had just won the lottery. The fact that his ecstatic expression made him even more attractive—and her cheeks heat up—made Briana seriously wonder if she had ever had control of the conversation at all.

At Carol's nod, she beckoned the two men after her, all the while feeling what were probably Taron's eyes boring into the back of her head, making the hair at the back of her neck stand on end. Once again, Briana clutched her shoulder bag's strap more tightly. She would have to be more careful in the next hour than she had ever had to be in her life.

She would be damned before she would allow a sexy smile and an intimidating demeanor bully her into giving up such a treasure without a legit reason.

CHAPTER THREE

*T*aron's eyes tracked Briana's every movement as keenly as a cat stalking a bird within grasp on the front lawn as she carefully pulled the book from its protective slipcase and placed it gently onto the examining table. It disturbed her to realize just how much his stare made her feel like that metaphorical bird.

Instead of studying the book last night, she should have spent the time looking up Taron Hildebrand on the internet. She was kicking herself that she hadn't thought until now to have Carol, at the very least, investigate whether or not Taron's appraiser really did own an auction company in New York before she had brought them to the back room. They could be a pair of con artists, for all she knew. It wouldn't be the first time someone used their good looks as a weapon...

CRISTINA RAYNE

Yeah, and maybe you just read too many thrillers, she thought sardonically.

However, there was no denying the man's rising excitement from the moment the book had first been revealed. If his story about the book being a family heirloom was true, she wondered just how long and hard he had searched, how much money he had spent, to find it.

"You hinted earlier that this book was written in an obscure alphabet," Briana said abruptly, breaking the loaded silence that had fallen between them. "Before I open this, can you tell me about the writing?"

He laughed. "*Very* obscure, yes, given that it's an alphabet created by my ancestors."

"Then—it was written in code?" she pressed.

"You could say that."

When it became apparent that no further explanation would be forthcoming, Briana decided to back off to something more innocuous in the hope that he would relax and open up a bit more. She had seen this type of reluctance in the past with a few of Carol's older clients, the determination to reveal nothing but what was absolutely necessary. Some families with ties back to various European nobility could be incredibly skittish about revealing too much history about the books—whether about the books themselves or a client's particular ties

24

to it—because they feared Carol would jack up the initial price.

"Sorry for the twenty questions," Briana apologized with faux sheepishness. "I'm a history major, so you must understand that finding a book as apparently old and intriguing as this one isn't one I'm eager to let go without a very good reason. Even then, at the very least, I would like to have my own curiosity sated."

Taron nodded, his eyes softening a bit. "I have a Ph.D. in history, myself, so I can well understand your reluctance to part with it, as well as your caution."

Briana leaned forward with both interest and suspicion. "Oh?"

"The Hildebrand family has been searching for generations for this book. Seeing my father and grand-father's frustration over the years as once promising leads turned cold over and over made me determined to be the one to find it. It also fanned the flames of my interest in the history of the times surrounding it."

He reached out a hand that quivered in either uncontainable excitement or fear of being wrong and stopped short of touching the front cover before Briana could yell at him about not touching it without gloves or at least a thorough washing.

"To finally, *finally* have it possibly within my grasp—it's indescribable."

"Did your studies include learning how to *read* it?" Briana found herself asking, unable to contain *her* excitement any longer despite her earlier determination to be as suspicious and cautious of the probable Englishman as possible.

His lips quirked up as he drew his hand back to his side. "Of course."

She picked up a new pair of white cotton gloves from the table and offered them to him. "Then I would very much like to hear you read the first page—if this is indeed your family's missing book, of course."

Taron eyed the gloves with a moue of distaste before he sighed and accepted them. "You know those aren't really necessary as long as you thoroughly wash and dry your hands with a fresh towel before handling the books, don't you?"

"I've heard," Briana retorted. "However, both Carol and I feel better using them if you don't mind."

"As you wish."

Carol came in with a tray containing three steaming tea cups just as Taron reached for the book, but she might as well have been a ghost for all either Taron or Mr. Brown paid any attention to her arrival. Without a word, the older woman headed for the small alcove in a back corner of the room that contained a circle of overstuffed chairs and a compact, wooden coffee table in the center and set the tray down. Briana had many fond memories sitting with Granny Ruth and Carol or regular patrons of the shop and friends sipping a cappuccino and discussing a new discovery or simply the latest bestseller.

Her eyes turned back to Taron. She regarded him speculatively as he carefully opened the book to what she thought was the title page while his appraiser moved in for a closer look. Maybe Taron wouldn't be averse to doing the same after examining the book.

Then Briana felt an inexplicable burst of adrenaline shoot through her system as Taron just—stilled. If the universe ever paused to take a breath, she would swear that cosmic moment between action and inaction would have exactly matched what she had just witnessed. It was almost as though she could feel the weight of that stillness down to her very soul, and if it weren't for the fact that she couldn't seem to move, couldn't seem to *breathe*, Briana would have stumbled away from him.

"Mr. Hildebrand? Is everything all right?"

Taron blinked at the sound of Carol's concerned voice, and that preternatural stillness instantly shattered. Suddenly freed from her strange paralysis, Briana had to lean hard against the edge of the table to keep legs that were now as wobbly as wet noodles from crumbling to the ground.

"...Forgive me," Taron murmured. He closed his eyes briefly before he turned to address Carol. "Although seeing the cover once again convinced me that I had indeed found the right book, seeing this..." He tapped the first line of strange symbols on the page lightly with his index finger. "...proved it beyond a shadow of a doubt, and I was overcome with emotions I was ill-prepared for."

You're not the only one, Briana thought shakily as she tried to pull herself together before Carol or either of their two guests noticed something was amiss with her.

What the hell had just *happened*? Sure, she had always been more sensitive to others' emotions than the average person, but she had never been affected like *this*. She had almost freaking collapsed, for God's sake!

Carol smiled kindly at him. "This sort of reaction happens more often than you would think. Where some see books as dusty old collections of pages, others see a priceless treasure."

Taron smiled wryly. "Or a precious heirloom in my case." His gaze lowered to the title page once again. " 'Herein lies the account of Beatrice Hildebrand regarding the happenings on the Ides of March.' " His eyes lifted, and Briana suddenly found her eyes captured in an intense, sunset-colored stare. "That's what this first page says—in somewhat modern terms, at least. This book is a narrative diary, penned by Beatrice's own hand about an incident that, to this day, has sparked many a passionate argument among my family about whether or not it actually occurred."

CHAPTER FOUR

Briana was so focused on Taron that it was a few seconds before she realized that she had heard the chiming of the shop entrance door's bells in the distance. Her eyes darted over to Carol, and her friend mouthed "I'll be right back" before heading back out into the main sales room of the shop.

"Would you—would you be willing to talk about that 'incident'?" she asked hopefully.

Taron's smile was suddenly all teeth. "Now that depends, Miss Wright," he said, his tone almost teasing.

"Right, of course," Briana replied with a wry quirk of her lips. "You're thinking about my refusal to sell you the book yesterday. Right now, I'm about ninety-eight percent convinced that the book truly belongs to you. If you can convince me about that final two percent, then I will be happy to just *return* the book to you."

He blinked, his features crinkling with blatant confusion. "You don't want any payment? Even considering that the book rightfully belongs to my family, I still wish to compensate you. I offered you five hundred thousand dollars yesterday. That offer still stands today."

It was Briana's turn to be utterly taken aback. "I found this book in my late grandmother's collection. I have yet to find any acquiring documents for it. My grandmother was a well-known rare books collector in this area. For all I know, it was donated to her. I know for a fact that she would've been ecstatic to be able to return an heirloom to you that you so obviously treasure. Taking your money just seems so—I don't know—*crass*."

"I see." Taron tilted his head and regarded her slightly for a few long seconds before exchanging a brief, unreadable glance with his appraiser.

Then, without another word, he reached a gloved hand over to the book and began to purposely, though still carefully, turn the yellowed pages until he came to the full-page drawing of the dragon head key she had been so excited to discover. There was no writing on the page, no annotations, just the drawing of the key, itself.

"According to my ancestor, Beatrice, this key was at

the center of that incident. To finally be able to read a first-hand account of it is worth my family's entire fortune to me."

Briana abruptly gasped as a momentous thought suddenly occurred to her. "You have it, don't you? The key!"

That shark-like grin once again appeared. "Come have dinner with me tonight at my hotel, and we shall see if that's true."

To say that Briana was blindsided by the invitation was the understatement of the century. She could feel the muscles in her face freeze in shock. Then in the next second, she mentally berated herself in disgust, and it was all she could do to keep her cheeks from heating up in embarrassment.

Idiot! There's no way someone who looks like a Greek god would be interested in you romantically. It was clear from the moment he first saw the book yesterday that getting his hands on it was his only goal. But still—

What was the harm of going? If accepting his invitation meant that she got to spend an evening eating good food, maybe drink a little wine, all while getting to ogle a gorgeous man, there was certainly nothing to complain about. Plus, as an added bonus, he might really have the key in the drawing and be willing to show it to her, to tell her the story that was allegedly in the book that he had teased so well, damn him.

"...but I thought Joseph was coming..."

The faint, muffled sound of Carol's voice coupled with the creak of the door behind her opening instantly shook her out of her thoughts. Crap! She had completely forgotten about Joseph coming to appraise the book.

She had only a split-second to process Carol's words and begin to wonder who her friend was talking to before Taron suddenly dashed past her and crashed shoulder-first into the door with a meaty thud, shutting it before it had even opened more than a few inches.

"What the hell are you *doing?*" Briana cried, instinctually backing up against the table as the click of Taron engaging the deadbolt on the door sounded out ominously in the air.

She then violently recoiled when Taron began to stalk towards her, jamming the small of her back painfully into the edge of the table and disorienting her long enough for him to firmly grab her upper arms. Yelling out in alarm, Briana immediately began to struggle against his hold with all her strength, ignoring the throbbing pain in her back as she tried to knee him in the balls.

However, she would have had better luck wrestling a

marble statue for all her efforts even phased him. Taron calmly regarded her with an expression that suspiciously looked like amusement as he held her imprisoned between his hands at arm's length, rendering her attempts to kick him laughably useless.

"Let. Me. *Go!*" Briana screamed angrily as she redoubled her efforts to try and twist out of his vise-like grip, but at that point, Taron wasn't even looking at her any longer, much less listening to her.

He was glaring in the direction of the door, his lips curled back into the beginnings of a snarl. The elegant, English gentleman was gone, and in his place was a man with a dark look in his already uncanny eyes that looked infinitely more unstable and scary.

A loud *thud* abruptly sounded out on the other side of the door as though someone had taken a sledgehammer to it, and Briana froze. Even in a panic, there was no way Carol would have been able to hit the door with that kind of force.

"There's a second door behind us! Take her! I'll distract him!" Mr. Brown ordered, moving around the table and heading towards the door with the determined, yet resigned, look of a man knowing he was about to die but wishing to meet his death head-on.

An undeterminable emotion flickered fleetingly within Taron's eyes before he nodded curtly towards the older man, and in the next breath, Briana was lifted and tossed over his shoulder into a fireman's carry before she could even think to struggle. She reflexively clutched at the back of his sport coat as he sprinted towards the back.

"I really hope this door leads outside and not a broom closet, or I'm about to cause more trouble for your friend," Taron said just as Briana heard the sound of a door splintering at the same time she felt a small jolt that caused a rock-hard shoulder to dig painfully up into her stomach.

She immediately began to kick her legs in renewed panic as the cool morning air hit her face. He had her *outside*! They were in a back alley between several buildings with not a single soul around.

"Dammit! Put me down, you asshole!" she screamed, pounding his back like a woman possessed.

Then the world did a one-eighty as Taron abruptly flipped her body back into a bridal carry. "Here, hold onto this, please," he commanded as Briana felt something hard land heavily onto her stomach.

She had already grabbed for the object on instinct before her gaze dipped down. She wasn't at all surprised to see the leather book that was at the center of all this craziness.

"I'm sorry for scaring you, but explanations will have

to wait," Taron said with a wry smile as she looked up at him sharply with half-frightened, half-pissed-off eyes.

What was strange was he really did sound genuinely sorry. That was the last coherent thought she had before her mind, as well as her body, completely froze as Taron's face began to—change.

What appeared to be the beginnings of large, oval-shaped and blood-red blisters began to rapidly swell up to about an inch above the entire surface of his tanned skin as though she were watching it happen in a time-lapse video. The large blisters were immediately followed by the hazel-orange of his eyes changing into a shade that was more the color of a wildfire under a blinding sun and his pupils stretching out until they resembled the narrow, vertical pupils of a cat.

Frozen in utter terror in his arms, Briana watched as, in a matter of a few seconds, his head began to both grow and change shape, his clothes ripping at the seams when his body also began to enlarge and contort into a new form. It was only when the pair of huge, red-membraned wings unfolded from his back and began to spread out to an impressive diameter and something rough and sharp tightened a bit unpleasantly around her upper torso and legs that she realized she was being held within the *talons* of an enormous red and black *dragon*.

A dragon that had only seconds before been a very human man.

With a single, powerful leap, the dragon shot up to the roof of one of the buildings. He stopped only long enough to fully extend his leathery wings to what had to be at least a jaw-dropping span of a hundred yards. Then with a couple of powerful flaps of those wings, they were airborne, and the force of their rapid ascent brutally pressing down on her body mercifully made her black out.

CHAPTER FIVE

It was the stomach-churning feeling of suddenly freefalling that jolted Briana awake. For a few, terrifying minutes she had no idea what the hell was going on as something enormous and roughly textured was pressing powerfully against the back of her head, forcing her face against a smooth, though hard, curved red surface that was almost hot enough to scorch her skin.

Then she heard what sounded like a cross between thunder and the crescendo of a crashing ocean wave in repeated intervals, and the vivid image of a pair of impossibly large, red and black leathery wings extended to their full span flashed through her mind.

Dragon.

Taron Hildebrand had shifted into a freaking dragon

before her very eyes, and she was now being carried away to God-only-knows-where-and-why by said dragon.

A very powerful urge to giggle at the utter absurdity of her current situation nearly overwhelmed her, but Briana closed her eyes tightly and took a few slow, deep breaths in an effort to stop the hysteria that was threatening to consume her mind. The *last* thing she needed to do right now was to fall into a blubbering mess of fear no matter how much she wanted to. If she wanted to survive this mother of all shit storms the universe had just rained on her, she needed her mind to be as clear and sharp as possible.

Becoming a dragon's appetizer was *not* the way she was going to go out, dammit!

Then her entire body jolted so violently that for a split-second, Briana was afraid her bones would shatter. Gritting her teeth, she forced her eyes open just as she was pulled away from where she had been pressed against what she now recognized was the dragon's chest. It was then that she got her first good glimpse of the dragon's body and realized what she had thought were large blisters forming on his skin were, in fact, a lattice of shiny *scales*.

A burst of hot, humid air abruptly washed over her from above, making Briana flinch and finally look up towards the creature's head with a mixture of curiosity and dread. His neck was long, sinewy, and covered with a thicker, more roughly-textured version of the huge red scales on his chest. His head and snout were that of a classic dragon, reptilian-like, with two long, crimson horns growing horizontally from his temples and only inches above his skull towards the back of his head. Each narrow, bony appendage ended in a wickedly sharp, black-tipped point.

His eyes—the deep oranges and yellows of the irises seemed to swirl in chaotic patterns as though she were looking deep into the heart of a raging wildfire. Staring into them was hypnotic, *dangerous.*

Briana jerked back within the confines of his talon-tipped hands and vigorously shook her head until the fogginess that had begun to inundate her mind from staring too long into his eyes dissipated. It was then that she finally noticed she was still somehow clutching the book with both hands.

The dragon opened his mouth, revealing a couple of rows of pointy, T. rex-sized teeth, and she was utterly shocked when a deep, booming voice emerged from within instead of the expected roar. "I'm setting you down now," he said with the same British accent he had as a human, blasting her with another gust of humid air that smelled of fresh ashes and something akin to the electrical smell of a live wire. "Please don't make me chase you."

Although it was probably a good sign that his breath didn't even remotely smell like rotting meat or even sulfur as she'd half-expected, Briana wasn't stupid enough to test his level of benevolence, especially with the implied threat in his last words.

Only when she felt her boots settle onto a hard surface did she dare to allow her eyes to flit briefly around at her surroundings. She had expected to see snow-capped mountains in the distance, the mouth of a cave, or even a vast, alien forest. The last thing she expected to see was a close-up of the sides of some very familiar buildings.

"You brought me to the roof of a building in the middle of downtown?" she blurted out.

"My hotel," he said in all seriousness, his eyes staring down at her keenly as though he expected her to bolt at any minute.

Briana threw her hands up in the air, a feeling of both relief and chagrin flooding through her. "That settles it. This whole crazy day *has* to be a dream. I'm probably drooling, passed out and facedown, on this weird book right now as we speak. Gorgeous men who transform into dragons are just too interesting to exist in our little old boring, mundane world."

The dragon who was once Taron nodded. "And we don't, but that's an explanation for a later time. I don't want to get ahead of myself, especially when you aren't even convinced that what's happening now is real, that *I'm* real and not just a figment of your imagination."

A surge of doubt began to creep into her mind. "This *can't* be real," she repeated stubbornly, hugging the book against her chest tightly. "It makes a hell of a lot more sense that what just happened is the result of my brain mixing up my memories of this book along with all the fantasy books and movies I've consumed to produce the most screwed up dream I've ever had rather than me standing here talking to a freaking dragon!"

Taron tilted his head in a manner so eerily similar to the way he had done it as a man that it sent a chill up Briana's spine and regarded her silently for a long moment. "Given how carelessly you're treating that book as opposed to how careful you were with it earlier, I think you really do believe that you're currently asleep. Well then, if you are so certain that this is a dream, why not seize the chance for a grand adventure? After all, what human can say that they have soared the skies with a firedrake?"

"*Firedrake?*" Her eyes immediately shot to his muzzle in alarm. "You actually breathe *fire*?"

The toothy grin he shot her was scary enough to

make her take a couple of instinctual steps away from him. "Would you like a demonstration?" he asked cheekily.

Shrugging with a nonchalance that she absolutely didn't feel, Briana replied, "Might as well get the full CGI package. Just—"

She trailed off, not liking where her thoughts were going. Still, if there was even a remote chance...

Briana swallowed against the lump of trepidation that had abruptly formed in her throat, and forced herself to continue, "Just don't burn anything down."

His eyes seemed to flash brighter. "Even if this is only a dream?" he taunted.

She lifted her chin mulishly. "Even if this is only a dream."

Taron opened up his giant maw wide, and a small burst of fire that was more red than orange shot out about a couple meters before dissipating harmlessly in the air. Briana had barely felt the temperature around her rise. It had probably been the equivalent of a human cough.

She was almost sure that the bastard was laughing at her inside, but she was secretly relieved. The more they talked, the more she was starting to doubt that she was, in fact, dreaming. If he was willing to humor her doubts this much, then if it did turn out that this terrifying but incredible creature indeed existed, maybe she didn't have to worry about becoming that dragon snack after all.

"Say I believe that I really am wide awake and this is all real," Briana said slowly, "that you're a dragon-shifter hunting for this book I found in my grandmother's collection only *yesterday*. What reason could you possibly have for scooping me up and flying me to the roof of your hotel building? My back was turned to the examining table. You could've easily snatched just the book and made a break for the back door. I somehow doubt it was because you needed someone to carry it for you while you flew."

"We might as well sit," Taron replied. "The answer to your question is a long one, and we are well hidden up here from prying eyes from down below."

He lowered and folded up his body onto the ground more gracefully and quietly than she thought a creature that large should be able to manage. He stretched out his arms before him, reminding her more of a cat settling down for a rest than anything reptilian.

"You look like a dragon guarding his treasure hoard," Briana couldn't resist saying, slowly lowering herself to sit on the cool concrete while never once taking her eyes off the curved, black talons at the end of his digits that were about the length of her torso.

She imagined one downward swipe could easily slice her in half from head to toe like warm butter. Yet—she really didn't think she had to worry about that. Other than lunging at her back at the bookshop and keeping her from kicking him where it counts, Taron hadn't behaved even remotely threateningly to her in the least. The fact that she was thinking about him as "Taron" and not "the dragon" was rather telling, as well.

"A building is quite a big keepsake to hoard," he quipped. "Unless you mean yourself, but how many stories of dragons have you read that have them hoarding humans?"

"Maybe a damsel or two, but I wouldn't be surprised if those kinds of stories also existed," Briana replied wryly. She then added with a wary frown, "You *aren't* planning on adding me to your collection, are you?"

Taron lowered his head until there was only about a foot of space between her and his snout, making her involuntarily flinch and her pulse speed up in sudden alarm.

"Would you honestly believe me if I said no?"

Swallowing thickly, Briana slowly shook her head. "I would be crazy not to have some small measure of doubt."

He pulled his head back and grinned that toothy grin that made something primal in her brain shudder.

"Good. That means you have great survival instincts. You may soon need them."

"Why?" she demanded suspiciously.

"I suppose that's as good a place to start explaining myself as any. You recall that the shop owner was about to bring someone into the room where we were examining Beatrice's book?"

Briana nodded. "Yeah. I thought it was Joseph, an appraiser from our circle. He works for an auction house in Dallas. I had invited him to come take a look at the book this morning, but from Carol's words—it was someone *you* knew, wasn't it? Is that why you charged the door like a crazed linebacker?"

Taron's eyes narrowed. "Oh, I knew him *very* well. That he's here in this world at all right now makes me both hopeful and fearful.

"In this world..." Briana repeated, her words trailing off at the implications.

"Of course. Did I not say that it was true that there are no dragons native to *this* world?"

"Then—how are *you* here?"

"According to you, a dream," he replied with a deep chuckle that made the air noticeably vibrate around her.

Briana scowled. She hated to admit it, but Taron did have a point. Not even she had dreams this convoluted and vivid. It really would be stupid to continue to delude herself.

"Fine. Laugh all you want," she growled, "but even *you* have to admit that me dreaming everything that just happened made more sense than me landing right smack in the middle of a fairytale."

"Fair enough," he agreed amiably, his tone somewhat mollifying her rising irritation.

"So?" she asked, looking up at him expectantly.

Taron tilted his head curiously at her before abruptly nodding. "Right. We were talking about the unexpected visitor in the shop…"

"…and how you came to this world," Briana reminded him, cringing inwardly at how ludicrous that sounded.

"The answers to both questions are interconnected," he said. "While I wish I had the time to explain the prologue to this tale more thoroughly, I'm afraid the person we left behind at the shop won't give us that luxury. Even so, I can't in all good conscience ask you to help me any further without giving you at least a truncated version of the story."

"Though you didn't exactly *ask* when you threw me over your shoulder like a sack of potatoes," Briana said dryly. "So that's why you didn't shift back into a man once you had me up here. You're running from that person. You want to be able to fly away without having to waste time shifting."

"I *am* sorry about that," Taron replied, sounding genuinely contrite, "but I didn't expect Cabak to track me to this city so quickly. Never mind the book, there was no way in hell that I was going to let that bloody bastard discover your existence. We're both extremely lucky that I got to you first."

"*Me?*" Briana exclaimed in bewilderment. "What the hell do I have to do with any of this? It's not like I could read anything in that book if that's what he was after."

"Maybe nothing or everything," he replied grimly. "The point is that Cabak would have snuffed out your life the moment he caught your scent."

Briana instantly jumped to her feet. "Scent? Wait! Don't tell me we just left my friend Carol alone with another dragon-shifter—no, that isn't important—with a potential *killer*!"

"Harold would have made sure she, at least, made it to safety," he assured her firmly.

Frantic with worry, it took her a long moment to remember that Harold was Taron's so-called appraiser. "Don't tell me your appraiser can shift into a dragon, too!"

Just how many dragons were now running around the world pretending to be human?

"No, just a very capable human and a dear friend."

Looking around, Briana spotted the building's rooftop door and started to step towards it. "I need to go back, anyway—hey!"

Between one blink and the next, Taron snatched her up into one giant fist and lifted her up to his eye level. Feeling as though she were trapped inside an uncomfortably tight and textured tube, rather than struggle futilely to free her arms, Briana settled on glaring at one of his enormous eyes.

"The best thing you can do for your friend is to stay away," he said frankly. "Cabak will have no doubt caught your scent from the shop. He will realize what I have found, recognize the potential danger, and think that I have fled the city to hide you away."

"You never did explain why he was after me in the first place," she said pointedly, trying to ignore the painful way one of the book's edges was digging into one of her boobs.

"It's because of your blood."

Briana stilled. "*What* about my blood?"

"It's very faint in you, but I would never in all eternity forget that scent. You share a bloodline with the witch that exiled me to this world."

CHAPTER SIX

*B*riana's first instinct was to shout out "that's insane!" The next was to stiffen as she felt a jolt of very real fear shoot through her body. Was *that* what this was all about? Not some old, weird book but trying to find the "witch" that possessed it to make her pay for what her alleged ancestor did to him?

"You want revenge." She was shocked at how utterly matter-of-fact her tone sounded.

That giant eye that filled her vision blinked slowly before he abruptly lowered her back to the ground and released her onto unsteady legs.

"That's not what I want from you at all."

Although every instinct within was screaming for her to run away, Briana forced herself to remain where she stood. Taron looked so taken aback by her accusation that she couldn't believe that he was lying to her. Who knew that a dragon's face could be so expressive?

She took a deep, calming breath. "Okay."

Taron's gaze sharpened as she once again lowered herself to sit cross-legged on the ground.

After a tense moment of silently staring at one another, Briana finally said, "Not that I'm ready to accept just yet that one of my ancestors was a real, spell-using witch from another world, but even if that's true, how does dropping that bombshell on me help you in any way? Because I can tell you right now that I don't have anything even remotely resembling a witchy power."

"As I said before, the answer to that question remains to be seen. All I ask right this moment is for you to hear me out. Then once I explain my situation, we will open Beatrice's book to the drawing of the key and see what the Fates have in store for both of us."

Briana suddenly had a strong urge to fling the book away. "What exactly do you think's going to happen?"

"What I 'hope' will happen," he corrected. "I hunted that book for nearly two centuries for the information that it contained. I even infiltrated the Hildebrand family and offered to aid them in their search for their lost heirloom. It was fitting, really, given that their surname is derived from words meaning fire, battle, strife, and sword. I never thought it would lead me to another of the *Ansi* blood, and make no mistake, you are of that bloodline, no matter how thin that blood has become within you. It's likely not a coincidence that your late grandmother had that book in her possession."

"My grandmother wasn't a witch, either, if that's what you're insinuating. She never would've kept something that important a secret from me."

But she didn't tell me about this book, did she?

Pushing that very uncomfortable thought away for the moment, Briana asked a bit crossly, "What do you mean, '*Ansi*' blood?"

"That's what we call non-dragon-shifters who can wield magic in my tongue," Taron replied. "Witch, mage, magician, wizard, warlock—those are the closest terms you humans have in this world. It's all interchangeable."

"Did the Hildebrand family know that you could shift into a dragon?"

"Of course. How else would I have been able to explain the fact that I don't age? We dragons are essentially immortal as long as we don't fall victim to violence. We are very hard to kill, but we still *can* be killed. I needed them entirely in the know to help me keep my secret from the rest of humanity over the long centuries, but I'm getting ahead of myself again. You need to understand the circumstances that led to my exile here.

"The history of my people spans across millennia, and I couldn't possibly explain every nuance of our society in such a short time. I suppose the most important thing you need to know is that there are four races of dragons in Elysia—my world—split two and two between the northern and southern hemispheres. For simplicity's sake, rather than use each race's name in my language, we'll just call them the firedrakes, stone dragons, water dragons, and ice dragons. For the most part, our peoples have lived together in relative harmony along with the non-shifters, but underneath that cooperation, the stone dragons have always resented the fact that our ruling monarchs for the northern hemisphere have always been firedrakes and only from the royal House of the Red Flame."

Briana sighed. "That sounds like the prologue to every attempted coup in history."

Taron grimaced. "Yes. Living here in this world over the last couple of centuries has taught me that lesson all too well, and that is, indeed, exactly what occurred. The highest ranking noble house among the stone dragons, the House of Blue Stone, convinced their people that they were strong enough, cunning enough, to take out the firedrake king and secure the throne. For the most part, they were correct."

"Wait! Don't tell me *you* are their king!" Briana exclaimed.

Her entire body was suddenly rocked by vibrations and gusts of hot dragon breath as Taron abruptly burst out laughing. "I'm sorry. It was a very valid conclusion to come to, but the look of incredulity on your face was priceless," he said, mirth making his eyes shimmer more brightly. "Do I not seem a king?"

His presence was certainly intimidating enough for a man used to wielding absolute power over his people, but he *was* a dragon after all. Her subconscious could have just as easily been reacting to the fact that the mother of all apex predators had been staring her down.

"Considering that you're the first dragon-shifter I've ever met, I wouldn't know one of your society's kings from the regular folk," she said with a huff. "I just couldn't help but think 'of course he is.' That the first dragon I meet is a dragon king just seems so absurdly cliché."

"Then you'll be happy to know that I am, in fact, *not* the king. I'm merely the second-born son of His Majesty, King Lyven of the House of the Red Flame. My true name is Astaron of the House of the Red Flame. The name

'Taron' was the closest I found to it in this world. At the very least, I didn't want to completely lose that small part of myself after having my home taken from me."

Briana looked at him sadly. "I can understand that. Should I call you Astaron, then?"

He shook his head. "Taron is fine. I've grown so accustomed to it over the centuries that I think of it as a true part of my name now, a nickname."

She nodded. "So, you're a prince? I'm not sure that bodes better for us given that you're still a member of the royal house. Royals are always a magnet for trouble."

Taron sighed, and she was taken aback at how deeply weary it sounded. "I can't argue with that."

The urge to comfort him rose up strong within her, and for a moment, Briana wished that he was in a form that she could easily show him some physical comfort, an empathetic squeeze on the shoulder or hand. Although she never in a million years would have done it, an image of her hugging his very nude body in comfort after he shifted back into a man rose unbidden in her mind. She was so startled by it, that she couldn't completely control the blush that briefly heated her cheeks.

What the hell was *wrong* with her?

If Taron noticed the extra color in her cheeks, he didn't let on with either expression or tone as he picked up the thread of his story again, "The head of the House of Blue Stone, Jathar, is the mastermind of the rebellion. He patiently waited for the time when either the king or the heir to the throne, my older brother Dagon, entered a period of Soul Sleep. Think of it like a bear entering hibernation. Only, instead of for the survival of a brutal winter, the Soul Sleep is our body and mind's way of coping with our immortality. For the firedrakes, the removal of that which helps fuel half of our life-force, our Dragon Fire, by a trusted family member is enough to send us into hibernation."

Suddenly, Taron rose up until he was sitting back on his haunches. Briana's eyes latched on to his right hand as he raised it to hover, palm up and level with the center of his chest.

Her eyes widened when what looked like a blood-red fireball exited his chest and settled down into the palm of his hand, undulating in a chaotic, pulsing pattern. She could feel the air around her warm up at least a few degrees even though she was a good twenty feet away from it.

"This is my brother's Dragon Fire. Without it, he has no hope of ever awakening."

"How long does a Soul Sleep last?" Briana asked, fascinated despite the grim direction his story had started to take.

"It's different for everyone. It can be as short as a decade to centuries, but the median time is usually fifty years."

"I can see how leaving yourself so vulnerable for so long can backfire for those in power."

Taron shook his head. "It may seem so to you, but those who enter their Soul Sleep are as protected by the king's guardsmen as the king, himself. We have a temple, a single, four-story tower located on the highest peak of a mountain range within my kingdom where every fire-drake goes to Sleep. The stone dragons have a similar temple of their own within a different range and equally as guarded. Even an army would not be able to break through their defenses very easily.

"But Jathar tried, anyway?" Briana hazarded.

"Dagon was ten years into his Sleep when the stone dragons made their play." She could hear the festering rage of that long-ago betrayal within those words. "We were led to believe by what we thought were several reliable sources deep within the heart of the House of Blue Stone that the plot involved the abduction of the Sleeping heir. While we scrambled to send a second army to supplement the army of troops already stationed at the tower, we were completely blindsided by the lone assassin that had slipped into the castle and succeeded in murdering the king. We have been at a stalemate ever since—trapped in an unending civil war, or at least that was the status before I was banished to this world."

"But you said your brother couldn't be woken up without his Dragon Fire and that he entrusted it to you," Briana said slowly. "With Dagon out of commission indefinitely and you trapped here, I can't imagine that the situation remained so black and white, us against them, that there wasn't at least a bit of infighting on your side about who would take up the seat of power in your absence. Would that have been enough to weaken the firedrakes' efforts to the point of losing?"

"This is where our own ancient laws of succession work against us even worse than you've guessed. There is a clause that covers even what was once the very unlikelihood of a coup during a ruling monarch's Soul Sleep. The usurper can legally claim the Dragon Throne as the de-facto king until the rightful ruler awakens and challenges the usurper king's authority in a fight to the death. He or she needs only to physically sit on the Northern Dragon Throne before the true heir. The fire-drakes must honor this or by law, risk losing the kingdom to the usurper forever. Fortunately, Jathar had yet to step foot within the palace at the time of my exile, and I pray that it has remained so."

"And I thought we had some bad laws..."

"It *is* forbidden to kill a dragon during the Soul Sleep," Taron said. "That's why the stone dragons' attempt to abduct the heir wasn't just a red herring to hide the fact that my father was the true target. With Dagon in their clutches and me, the holder of his Dragon Fire, banished to another realm with no real hope of ever returning, the only way to unseat the usurper from rule once he physically claimed the throne would be to kill not only Jathar but every last dragon from the House of Blue Stone and retrieve Dagon before the stone dragons can kill him out of vengence."

"How in the world did you get banished here in the first place?" Briana asked. "I know you said it was a witch, an *Ansi*, that did it, but I have a hard time wrapping my head around the concept. Did she open up a portal between worlds with a spell or something and push you through?"

Taron growled. "Yes. That's exactly what happened. I was in the form of a man when I was betrayed by a once-trusted *Ansi* within the tower while trying to return my brother's Dragon Fire to him after the king was assassinated."

"Obviously, a witch came to this world since you insist that I have witch blood. Was it her? The one who betrayed you?"

"No. Though from the same bloodline, the *Ansi*

blood within you smells ancient, very far removed from hers. Although long-lived, the *Ansi* aren't immortal. Perhaps your ancestor was also exiled to your world long ago, though I suppose we'll never learn the truth. No, that witch is very much dead given that I managed to fry her to a crisp before I fell completely into the portal she and another had created."

"You said you were in your human form when you fell through the portal. You can breathe fire without being in your dragon form?"

"I'm not sure if 'human' is the correct way to describe my other form, but yes, I can very easily breathe fire in that form, too."

Briana shrugged. "If it looks like a human and walks like a human…"

"The people in this world *do* smell very much like the non-shifters of Elysia, so who's to say we all don't share a common ancestry? However, that's a discussion for another time."

"I can't imagine what it must've been like to pop up into an alien world, not able to communicate with anyone."

"The portal was connected to an actual, physical doorway in this world located inside an English castle. The moment I stumbled across the threshold and turned around to see not the portal, but a darkened bedchamber with strange furnishings, I knew I was well and truly trapped here. The ability of some of the more powerful *Ansi* to cross into other realms was well known, so I damned well knew what had just happened to me.

"However, instead of wallowing in despair or rage, I immediately set out to learn the customs and language of the people I now found myself living among in the hope of trying to discover a way to reconnect that door to my realm. I searched out every whisper, every whiff of magic, but for years, I found nothing even remotely close to what I needed. Then sometime in the mid-eighteen hundreds, I heard talk of a legend in a small English village in the north.

"A key had appeared out of seemingly thin air, one that had opened up 'a door to paradise.' At least one woman had disappeared across its threshold, never to be seen again. With an actual object to seek, I started to quickly discover snippets of the same story all across the British Isles. It was only through piecing together these small anecdotes of lore that I finally heard the story of a woman named Beatrice Hildebrand who had allegedly entered a 'doorway to heaven' after a glass-like key with a dragon's head appeared in her hands one night. What made her story so intriguing was that she allegedly returned back home."

Briana sucked in a sharp breath, and her gaze immediately fell to the book still resting on her lap. "Now I see why you wanted this book so badly."

"It was said that her accounts of her time in the other world were bound into a leather volume that had been passed down as an heirloom until the early 1800s when it inexplicably disappeared from all records. One thing those accounts told me was the dragon key unlocks the door on both sides. I hoped to verify that point through Beatrice's own words when I found her book."

Suddenly Taron's grin was full of teeth. "Not to mention, Beatrice Hildebrand was a descendant of an *Ansi*—the same *Ansi* as you."

CHAPTER SEVEN

"*T*hat can't be right," Briana protested instantly, her pulse racing with something like fear. "Granny Ruth and I have traced our family tree back to the 1700s, and there wasn't a single Hildebrand among our ancestors!"

"Given how weak that particular bloodline has become in you, I'm not surprised," Taron replied, sounding unconcerned. "I've occasionally run across others of that bloodline all across the world during my endless search, and I doubt their familial ties could have been easily linked without an extensive DNA analysis. Your original *Ansi* ancestor could have arrived here during the reign of the pharaoh, Khufu, for all we know. As I said before, the *Ansi* blood I smell within you is ancient. Imagine how widespread his or her progeny must be after thousands of years."

"Even so, I still don't understand why my having witch blood from another world is important to you. If you're hoping that I can somehow cast the same spell that witch used to banish you here, then I'm afraid you're just going to be disappointed."

Briana opened the book to a random page, a little surprised to see the picture of the dragon key. Taron's gaze lowered to the now opened book in her lap.

He raised a hand and carefully poked at the drawing with the tip of one, black talon. "What I need from you isn't a spell. What I need, what I'm hoping with all my soul that you can give me, is this key, a key that once opened a door to my world, to Elysia."

Feeling her heart sink, Briana reached a hand to that enormous talon and carefully laid her palm onto its shiny surface. She was a bit surprised that it was warm. She had expected it to feel rough like bone, but instead, it was as though she were touching a talon carved from pure obsidian.

"So that's it," she said softly, looking up at him with sympathy despite what she was about to say. "You were just toying with me when you hinted that you had the dragon key from the drawing because you've believed since the first day you met me that not only did I have Beatrice's book, but also the key."

Briana raised an eyebrow when he shook his head. "I'm pretty confident you don't."

She frowned, now feeling utterly confused. "Why?"

"Because you're currently here with me," Taron replied simply, "and looking at that picture should have incited a stronger emotion than just the curiosity you've shown."

Her frown deepened. "I don't follow."

Taron stared down at the place where her hand rested against his talon for a long, uncomfortable moment. Finally, with a heavy sigh, he abruptly pulled his hand back, startling her. The expression in his eyes was suddenly unreadable.

"Taron, what—"

And then she felt it, something hard, cool, and smooth beneath her left hand that still rested where it had fallen on the vellum page when Taron had pulled his hand away so unexpectedly. Briana yanked her hand away with an oath, the book nearly falling off her lap with the sudden movement.

Without warning, a humongous dragon's snout flooded her vision, his T. rex looking teeth mere inches away from her face. She flinched so hard that she nearly fell backward. The smell of ashes inundated her senses as gust after gust of almost too-hot-to-bear dragon's breath washed over her as he seemed to be hyperventilating.

"It's here! It's here!" Taron roared, making Briana wince and cover her ears in pain in response to the extra decibels at such close range. "You did it! You *did it!*"

Did what? she thought dazedly, sure that everyone in the whole state had heard his shouting.

"Quickly! Pick it up. I dare not touch it."

"Pick what up?"

"The key of course! The dragon key."

The giant dragon head disappeared from her field of vision, and only then did Briana slowly remove her hands from her ears. They still rang from taking the full brunt of his booming voice.

"Forgive me," Taron said, his voice back down to an infinitely more tolerable volume. "I didn't mean—in my excitement—but the key—"

Briana automatically followed his gaze back down to the book in her lap, and her eyes widened when she saw a semi-opaque key about four inches long with a three-dimensional, horned dragon's head and two delicate-looking teeth wedged into the crease of the book, a key that looked impossibly like the drawing beside it.

A key that had *not* been there moments ago.

"What in the world…" she said weakly, unsure if anything would ever make sense again.

"Please take it," Taron pleaded. "Take it before it disappears. Quickly!"

It was the look of absolute desperation in his eyes that had Briana scooping up the key despite not wanting to touch it at all. Once it was in her hand, Taron all but collapsed onto his belly and closed his eyes, looking so exhausted that it made her throat tighten with emotion.

"I thought this day would never, *never* come," he admitted roughly.

"I don't understand. What the hell just happened?" Briana asked, eying the key in her hand as though she were holding a sleeping viper.

It was more substantive than she had expected, perhaps weighing around a pound.

"The key only appears to the one that's meant to use it during a great time of need," Taron said, "That is its lore. Now I can go home. Now I can save Dagon and restore order to my kingdom once again."

"Um—I hate to be a wet blanket, but how do you know that it'll unlock the door that leads to *your* world? You said the stories about the key talked about various people opening a door to paradise or heaven. That could mean anything and anywhere."

Taron opened his eyes and slowly grinned. "Because *I* found you, and the key appeared."

"That's it?" Briana asked incredulously. "*That's* your logic?"

"There's also the fact that Beatrice wrote the book in the language and alphabet of my people."

She had completely forgotten that Taron had been able to easily read the strange writing.

"Okay…so what now? I stick this key in the nearest lock, and the door will just open up to Elysia?" she asked skeptically. "Just like that?"

"It was my thought to use it on the door whose threshold I initially fell across two hundred years ago to enter this world. My gut tells me that is the correct path."

"Your 'gut' tells you, huh? Maybe you should read this book some more before we do anything," Briana suggested wryly. "For all you know, this might be a one-shot deal."

"We?"

Briana snorted as she stuffed the key into the right, front pocket of her jeans. Magic key or not, just touching the thing made her extremely uneasy.

"Of course I'm going to help you, you big lizard."

Flashing her a chastising look, Taron pulled himself back up onto his haunches. "Then this 'big lizard' will fly us directly to England right now. The castle I appeared in is currently empty as well as owned by me. I needed to make certain that the door and its lock were preserved. We can study the contents of the book there while that bugger, Cabak—"

A rapid narrowing of his eyes was her only warning before Briana was suddenly snatched up roughly by one red hand, followed by a deafening crash behind her that sounded as if the building were cracking open. She looked over her shoulder in enough time to see a large boulder hurtling towards them, a dark mass of blue a shade lighter than the surrounding sky blotting out the sun behind it. A split-second later, the world became a jumbled mess of blues, reds, tans, and grays as she was jerked around in several different directions until she felt as though her neck would snap. Taron's hand also squeezed her just a bit too hard and made it difficult to breathe.

Then the world just as abruptly became upright again, and though dizzy, Briana was at least able to breathe more easily—for about two seconds. A stream of orange-red fire a million times more powerful and impressive than his earlier demonstration shot out from Taron's maw, instantly heating the surrounding air. Her lungs felt as though they were being scorched when she involuntarily gasped.

Her arms trapped once again within Taron's fist, Briana tried to protect her face from the heat by pressing it closer against the smooth scales of a giant index finger. Then the brutal heat was suddenly gone, and another huge, red-scaled hand formed a cover over her head, plunging her into darkness.

"Speak of the Devil and of course he comes," Taron snarled. The sound of vigorously flapping wings reached her ears even through the insulation of the hands around her, followed by a violent jerk upwards that made her teeth snap together painfully. "Looks as though that trip to England will be a tad bumpy, after all."

With both the skin on her face and the lining of her lungs feeling tight and burning with pain, Briana could only lay the side of her head against a few of his scales, squeeze her eyes shut, and groan miserably, wondering if her face now resembled a boiled lobster. She was also keenly aware of the dragon key in her pocket digging sharply into her upper thigh, reminding her mockingly of her agreement to help Taron get back to his homeworld.

Considering she had just been in the middle of a freaking fight between two monstrously enormous *dragons*, she had come out of it relatively unscathed. How close had she come to becoming a wet, chunky stain in the concrete by the massive boulder that other blue dragon had thrown at her? She was damned lucky that she had come out at the other end of a battle that included literal streams of fire and rocks the size of a house with nothing worse than what would probably amount to the equivalent of a sunburn.

Now would be a good time for me to wake up, she thought with a choked laugh.

Too bad the pain in her body pretty much guaranteed she wasn't asleep.

CHAPTER EIGHT

For the first hour of the flight, Briana endured sudden, stomach-churning drops and lightning fast ascensions that made her nearly pass out with the added g's of force. She even thought she heard the crackling roar of Taron shooting fire from his mouth a couple of times, which meant that they had yet to shake the blue dragon from their tail.

Then after a long while of steady flying, Taron carefully maneuvered her a bit higher until she could see a portion of one fiery-colored eye through a small gap between a couple of the fingers he had cupped over her head for protection.

"Are you all right?" he rumbled over the sound of his wings flapping and the whistling of the wind as they sliced through the air.

"I am now that the horribly bumpy rollercoaster ride seems to be over," she shouted, unsure if he could even hear her puny voice. How keen was a dragon's hearing, anyway? "Was the dragon that attacked us what's-his-name that came looking for you in the bookshop?"

"Cabak," Taron growled, the utter loathing in his voice practically tangible.

Yep, he could hear her just fine, which was a relief. At least if they could talk, it would take her mind off her discomfort and the surge of claustrophobia she was beginning to feel at being unable to move her arms and legs with very little light shining through between his fingers.

"I've managed to lose him for now," he said, "but that means we'll have to take the long way around to the castle."

"Won't that be the first place he goes looking for us?"

"Only the Hildebrands know that I own it. I used a fictitious name when I purchased it and haven't stepped foot in it since Cabak entered this world two years ago."

"Should we expect more dragon-shifters to come after us?" Briana asked worriedly.

"No—at least for the moment. Until Cabak appeared before me, there were no other dragons present in this world."

"That you know of," she said. "Just look at how many old myths about dragons we have all over the world. Now that I've met a real honest-to-God dragon, I don't think that's a coincidence. Either dragons have been coming here from your world for ages, or they came long ago and stayed long enough for stories of them to be passed on."

"Only the *Ansi* have the power to open portals to different realms," Taron said, sounding troubled. "If dragon-shifters have been coming to your world, then they are doing so with their aid in absolute secrecy."

"If I were you, I would keep a closer eye on the *Ansi* when you get back to your world," Briana said dryly. "It seems they may be up to a lot of sketchy things besides stabbing the firedrakes in the back. I wouldn't think a group powerful enough to travel to different worlds would be satisfied being ruled by anyone, even someone as powerful as a fifty-foot-tall fire-breathing dragon. Maybe they really haven't sided with the stone dragons in your civil war. Their actual reason for helping to incite the war could've been to weaken both sides enough to stage a coup of their own."

Taron fell silent for a long moment. Briana almost regretted her words. Having a potential second usurper come into the picture had likely never entered his mind, and now that she had pointed it out, she had just added something else for him to worry about along with his mountain of other worries.

"Perhaps the Fates have heard my pleas after all," he said finally, an odd note in his tone. Then he asked a bit more sharply, "You *do* still have the dragon key?"

Yeah, it's giving my thigh a new bruise as we speak.

Briana frowned. Although she hadn't had the time or the desire to study it more carefully before she had banished it into her pocket, at first glance and feel, the key had appeared to be made from a glass-like substance. Should they be worried that it could crack given how firmly it was being pressed between Taron's scaly hands and her body?

"I didn't drop it if that's what you're worried about," she retorted, "but you might want to ease up on the squeezing if you want the key to make it to England in one piece."

"I'm more worried about it disappearing. I ran across more than one story that claimed the key was indestructible—at least by fire, sword, or blunt force."

Although he probably couldn't see her face properly through the crack of his fingers, she scowled at his eye, nonetheless. "After all the trouble you went through to get the damned thing, do you *really* want to test that theory? Besides, I think my legs have gone numb."

She was relieved to feel the pressure around her body lessen slightly. "Better?" he asked, amusement coloring his tone.

"Not really, but I just realized that we're probably somewhere close to orbit right now, and I'd rather not risk literally slipping through your fingers and falling to my death."

He chuckled. "We aren't quite that high up. Although traveling at a higher altitude would shave a few hours off our journey, a human like you would both freeze to death—despite the extra warmth radiating off my hands—or suffocate at those kinds of elevations."

"Oh, right…" Briana replied with a grimace. "But— aren't you worried about showing up on someone's radar?"

"My scales prevent that."

When it became apparent that he wasn't going to elaborate, she decided to let it go in favor of a more pressing concern. "So, where are we right now?"

"We're nearly clearing Antarctica."

"What the hell are we doing in Antarctica?"

Somehow, she had thought "taking the long way" meant going across the Pacific rather than the Atlantic Ocean.

"I managed to ground Cabak in the Caribbean. I saw a storm brewing towards the south, and the added ozone in the air was just the thing I needed to disrupt my scent trail. I'm hoping he believes that I'm trying to get you back to my penthouse in New York, or at the very least, not even consider the possibility of me flying this far south. With any luck, we'll be in England in about an hour."

"An *hour*? Just how fast can you fly?"

"Not quite as fast as Superman," he replied cheekily.

A surprised laugh burst from her lips. "Hearing a *dragon* talk so casually about a comic book character is just plain weird."

"I'll have you know that I *adore* reading comics," Taron said in a particularly posh accent. "Although, Batman has always been my favorite."

"Me too!"

It was in this vein, finding out that Taron was very much serious about loving to read comics—a hobby she also shared—and pretty much nerding out about various comic storylines that they passed the time during the rest of their flight. Not once did they bring up the dragon key, Cabak, or even Beatrice's book. When he abruptly announced that they were coming up to his castle, Briana was genuinely shocked at how quickly the time had passed and how easily he had made her forget the throbbing in her slightly-singed face and her discomfort of not being able to move anything other than her neck.

"If it's safe, can you remove your top-most hand so I can see it?" Briana asked.

"Of course. Just let me descend a bit more, first."

A few seconds later, she felt her stomach drop as Taron rapidly descended and then was momentarily blinded as he removed the hand that had formed a protective dome over her head. It was probably around four in the afternoon, London time.

Briana hissed and blinked rapidly as her eyes started to water. She struggled against the massive dragon hand curled around her body for a long, frustrating moment until she managed to pull her left arm free to rub the tears from her eyes vigorously.

Sitting in the center of a sprawling estate with lots of trees and surrounded on all sides by farmland, Taron's castle looked, to her immense delight, just as she expected it to. It was a weathered, medieval fortress of light gray stone with five square towers of various widths and heights and around a six or seven-foot perimeter wall surrounding the entire structure.

"Wow. It's gorgeous! I suppose it fits that it's owned by a prince."

Taron snorted. "You should see my kingdom's royal

palace. Most of it is a fortress carved into the side of a mountain. One of the ballrooms, alone, would dwarf the whole of this structure."

Briana rolled her eyes as Taron flew over the perimeter fence and landed on the front lawn only a few feet away from the entrance. "Yep, definitely a spoiled prince," she teased.

Another snort as Taron carefully set her down onto the cobblestone driveway in front of a short, stone staircase leading up to the front door. "Dragons are not spoiled."

Luckily for him, she was too busy trying to keep her numbed legs from collapsing from under her to retort. They were already starting to hurt something fierce with that pins and needles sensation she hated.

Then she did fall over onto her rump in surprise as the huge, red firedrake began to contort and shrink in front of her. Within seconds, a black-haired man covered from head to toe in shiny, red scales stood before her—a very *naked*, very *well-endowed* man with the muscular body of an athlete. Briana froze, so completely caught off guard that a gear in her brain seemed to have gotten stuck in mid-thought.

The scales seemed to rapidly sink directly into his skin until only his tanned, human skin remained. Even the pupils of his eyes had rounded until she was staring with wide eyes into the same sunset-colored eyes she had first seen in Carol's bookshop.

A slow, cat-like smile stretched his lips. "Like what you see?"

Shaking her head and laughing, Briana accepted the hand-up he offered, careful to keep her eyes above the waist. However, she couldn't resist ogling his chest muscles just a little bit.

"You're awful!" she scolded. "I hope you have at least a pair of pants stashed away here."

His wicked grin widened. "We'll just have to see, won't we?"

It was strange to hear him speak with his human voice. She had gotten so used to the dragon in the past couple of hours that it was almost just as weird to see the gorgeous man of before that had intimidated her so much. It made some of her early shyness return with a vengeance, and she couldn't quite keep from blushing just a little bit. He had absolutely no shame at all.

He barked a laugh. "Come on," he said as he absently threaded their fingers together without a moment's hesitation and led her up the stairs. "It's much too cold out for us to be standing in the driveway any longer when a large hearth awaits us inside."

She doubted very much that a firedrake, whether in his human form or not, ever got cold. This had to be the first time in history a conversation about comic books had led to a man as drool-worthy as Taron to feel comfortable enough with a woman he had just met— one that he had kidnapped, no less—to treat her as though they had been friends for years just as he was now.

"Um, I hope you have a spare key lying around here," Briana said in an effort to distract herself from the heat of his hand around her own.

Who was she kidding? It was to distract *her* from the naughty voice inside that was urging her to sneak a peek at his naked ass. She was a butt girl, through and through.

I can't believe I'm lusting after a guy that's technically a dragon!

Taron gave her a thumb's up with his free hand. "This is my key."

Belatedly, she noticed that in place of a deadbolt lock was a small, black touchscreen just large enough for him to press his thumb against. The history buff in her was a bit outraged that he had added such a modern piece of tech like a thumbprint scanner on a centuries-old castle instead of just using the original lock and key.

Just thinking about keys made her once again acutely

aware of the dragon key hidden away in her pocket. If the castle had indeed required a key that Taron obviously didn't have, being as naked as he was, would he have suggested she use the key then? Just the thought of using it made her stomach sink with dread. Suddenly, a biometric lock didn't seem so sacrilegious anymore.

CHAPTER NINE

*B*riana watched in fascination as a now mercifully fully-clothed Taron shot flames from his mouth onto the stack of logs and paper kindling in a fireplace so huge that she, at five-foot-five, could have walked into it without having to duck her head down very much. However, just because he was now wearing a pair of jeans, it didn't mean that she didn't take the opportunity while he was bending down tending to the fire to appreciate how well those hard, round globes filled out those jeans.

And she accused *him* of being awful...

Before he caught her staring, Briana forced herself to turn her attention to Beatrice Hildebrand's book that was currently opened to the first full page of that strange writing. Taron had promised to read it aloud to her, and Briana couldn't help feeling a growing excitement.

Despite every crazy and terrifying thing that had happened to her today, she had to admit that she was looking forward to learning exactly what had happened to Beatrice when she had used the dragon key to literally open a door into Taron's world. What she must've thought seeing a dragon soaring in the sky for the first time…?

"My guess is that she ended up within an *Ansi* dwelling," Taron said abruptly as he sat down on the sofa with only inches between them, startling her from her thoughts. "Being a descendant, she would've been welcomed with open arms, especially if they knew or at the very least, had an inkling of who her ancient ancestor—*your* ancestor—had been. Perhaps it was even she who showed them the way to your world again."

"You're *sure*, absolutely sure, that I have *Ansi* blood?" Briana asked for the millionth time.

"Positive. It's like the scent of a lightning bolt, metallic and full of power; the fragrance is unmistakable."

Unsure of how she felt about being part alien-witch, she let the issue go for the moment, one of a thousand different things on her "to-examine-later" list. "Okay, okay. So, are you going to read the whole book or…?"

"As much as I would like to, I don't believe we shall have that luxury," Taron said, his expression suddenly grim. "Although I *think* that I muddied our trail enough, it really is only a matter of time before Cabak finds us. That he's here in this world at all means that the stone dragons have become desperate, either because they have failed to break through the defenses of the tower where Dagon Sleeps to claim his body even after all these years at a significant loss to their forces, or as you suggested, the *Ansi* may have taken him instead. Perhaps the *Ansi* plan on capturing *me* in order to acquire Dagon's Dragon Fire to use as a bargaining chip."

"The intrigues of monarchies and their enemies make my head hurt," Briana groaned. "What exactly are you hoping to find in the book? I'll listen for clues you might miss while you read it to me."

"A confirmation," he replied. "Before you attempt to use the dragon key, I need to know whether or not Beatrice returned to this realm from the same door she used to enter mine."

"Ah, I see, but considering that I'm the one—"

Without warning, the entire wall behind them crashed inward, shoving a wave of dust and rock towards them and nearly making Briana bite her tongue as she instinctually dove forward across the coffee table, her body propelling the book onto the floor along with her. Coughing violently as she tried to breathe through a cloud of dust, she only had enough time to raise her head and glimpse the large body of what looked like a blue, stone sculpture of a dragon suddenly come to life before a pair of muscled arms as hard as steel wrapped around her middle and jerked her backward towards a side door.

Rather than scales, the texture of the blue dragon's body was very similar to the large blocks that had been used to build the castle. A stone dragon. Cabak...

Once across the threshold, Taron wasted no time scooping her up into his arms and sprinting down a long, dark hallway. His hair was almost entirely gray with dust as well as sprinkled across his face. However, the hazel-orange of his eyes seemed to ignite into literal flames as they raged with his anger.

He cleared the narrow staircase at the end of the hall in two bounds and raced to the left down another hallway full of tapestries whose designs blurred altogether in chaotic swirls of color as they sped by. Another turn to the right at the end of that hallway and Taron slid to a halt in front of a thick, wooden door in the center.

"We don't have much time," he growled urgently as he set her down on her feet. "Use the key in this door!"

"Right!" Briana rasped, digging a hand into the front

pocket of her jeans as the castle walls shook violently once again. "But where—what if I do something wrong—"

Taron grabbed her shoulders tightly. "Listen to me. The dragon key appeared in *your* hand. Your ancestors came from my world. I can only hope the Fates will unlock this door and reveal the place where we need to go, the place that, in a way, we *both* originated from. The original 'door' within the fabric of our worlds my *Ansi* betrayer opened and thrust me through."

She nodded curtly in sudden understanding. "The door to the tower where your brother hopefully still Sleeps."

"*Astaron!*" Cabak roared, so loudly that Briana was afraid that her eardrums would rupture.

However, she didn't drop the key to cover her ears like she desperately wanted to. Instead, she gritted her teeth and scrambled to thrust it into the keyhole, amazed when it actually went in smoothly without the slightest resistance.

The floor beneath them started to crumble after another crash shook the walls around them. Briana let go of the key and cried out in alarm as she began to fall down into a huge crack that had formed between the stones under her right foot. Taron grabbed her left arm and jerked her back flush against his front.

"Turn it *now*!" he shouted.

Briana grabbed the dragon head sticking out of the lock and gave it a sharp turn, half-afraid that she would break it. A loud *click* sounded out amidst the cracking and rumbling of the castle being demolished around them by a rampaging stone dragon, echoing louder than was natural. It was a reverberation she swore she could feel in her very bones.

Then Taron all but shoved her against the door just as she turned the doorknob, his body heavy at her back, and before she knew what was happening, they were both falling forward onto a red and black woven rug littered with strange symbols, Taron landing onto her back.

Her head swimming with a sense of vertigo, Briana tried to make sense of her surroundings. Her first instinct was to panic. Crap, did the key not work? Her next was to panic for a completely different reason. What if the key *did* work?

She had never intended to follow Taron across the threshold into Elysia. In fact, she had never even gotten past the thought of opening the portal, much less how she expected to get back home from a country she had entered without a passport or going through customs.

Briana instantly froze when the blade of a sword appeared mere inches from her nose, and a deep voice spat out a string of unintelligible words above her, angrily. Then Taron was shouting urgently near her ear in some weird, guttural language, and suddenly her vision was flooded by several pairs of darkly-clothed legs rushing towards them.

"Taron!" she cried out in alarm, wondering what the hell was going on, wondering if she was about to die.

The weight on her back vanished, and Briana suddenly found herself in Taron's arms again, her back pressing into his front. His arms were steel bands around her waist as though he was afraid she was going to dash away.

"It's all right," he said into her hair just as she finally got a good look at her surroundings.

Briana gasped as she realized that they were in a dimly lit room with gray, stone walls. The only illumination came from a series of blazing torches that cast shadows over the bed they encircled, as well as over the bodies of at least a couple dozen black-haired men and women dressed in identical black tunics with thick red threading along the cuffs and seams that were surrounding Taron and her. Most held swords, but a few were aiming a wooden, crossbow-like weapon directly at them.

"Uh—what part of this picture is all right?" she hissed.

"Everything," Taron replied in a strange tone. Then he let out a joyous whoop before she could even open her mouth to reply and tightened his arms around her in a back-breaking hug. "After two centuries of exile, I'm finally *home.*"

CHAPTER TEN

*B*riana had known before she craned her neck over her shoulder so fast that her neck popped loudly that she was completely and utterly screwed.

The staircase that descended into an eerie gloom from the threshold of the door she and Taron had just fallen through just confirmed it, if not the fact that an unnerving silence had replaced the sound of a castle being destroyed by a pissed off stone dragon. She could hear her own breathing more keenly than she ever could before, short, gasping, and *panicky,* while her heart was beating fast enough to send her into cardiac arrest.

Shit.

"It's there, right?" she whispered. "The key—it's still there in the keyhole, right?"

She felt Taron stiffen against her before he gave her another squeeze around the middle, this one reassuring. "It is."

Briana let out the breath she hadn't realized she was holding and sagged with relief in his arms. The dragon key was still there. Maybe she wasn't as screwed as she had thought.

Now that she wasn't on the brink of freaking out, she finally remembered that they had a rather sizable audience and the likely reason why.

"Is that Dagon on that bed?" she asked tentatively.

Taron released her and stepped forward. "Yes," he replied, that one word steeped with a plethora of emotions.

That single step shattered the stillness that had fallen over everyone else in the room, and within two beats, Taron was mobbed like a celebrity suddenly spotted by paparazzi. A flurry of words, laughter, and embraces were exchanged, and even though Briana couldn't understand a word of it, pure joy was universal, and seeing that emotion on Taron's face made her feel choked up as well.

As she stood apart from the celebration, feeling awkward and unsure but nonetheless happy for Taron, she remembered the dragon key that Taron had assured her was still sticking out of the keyhole in the door behind her. A quick glance over her shoulder confirmed it. While she was being ignored, Briana hurried over to the door and pulled out the key, deliberately ignoring the fact that the key was now so cold that it actually burned her skin like dry ice when she touched it. She shoved it back into her pocket and vigorously wiped her hand on the side of her jeans to get rid of the sting.

When Taron finally turned around, sunset eyes seeking her, she was back in the spot he had left her as though she had never left it, staring back at him uncertainly. She had been tempted to try to use the key on the other side of the door while his back had been turned and everyone else was distracted, but what stopped her was the possibility that the door in her world may no longer exist thanks to Cabak. Between the thought of opening a door that led into a dimensional void or sticking with Taron, who just might be able to lead her to an *Ansi* still loyal to the firedrakes who could safely open a portal back home for her, it was a no-brainer.

"Come," Taron beckoned with a crook of his fingers. "I've explained to the royal guard your role in getting me back to this world. You have as much right to see this as they do."

"See what?" Briana asked as she approached him cautiously.

She was surprised when he reached down and took

her right hand in his left and led her through the crowd of guards, who instantly parted like the Red Sea, to the bed in the center of the room. At first glance, the Sleeping dragon-shifter looked dead. Dagon was outfitted in a thick, black tunic embroidered in gold thread in an elegant, stylized flame pattern and black breeches made from a linen-like material. He even had on a pair of black, knee-high leather boots. His hands lay with fingers intertwined in the center of his chest. A narrow crown of golden flames also encircled his head. He looked like a monarch laid out in the best of his finery for a state funeral, striking against the crimson coverlet.

He also looked remarkably like Taron, giving her an unpleasant flash of *déjà vu* of seeing Granny Ruth lying in her coffin in the chapel of the funeral home. To see someone so familiar in a remarkably similar state again gave her a chill and made her heart clench with remembered grief.

"He doesn't look like he's even breathing," Briana murmured in dismay.

Taron squeezed her hand. "That's because he's not," he replied. "When I removed his Dragon Fire, his body fell into a near state of suspended animation. This is the only time a dragon's mind can completely rest as we don't sleep."

"You don't sleep even when you're in the form of a man?" she asked incredulously.

He shook his head. "We naturally have an overabundance of energy due to the nature and power of our Dragon Fire. Thus, our bodies don't need sleep to recharge or repair themselves like humans or even the *Ansi*."

"Dragons really are incredible," Briana said with a hint of awe.

Taron smirked. "Yes, we are." He released her hand and stepped closer to the bed. "However, our Dragon Fire is something even more magnificent."

This time, he held out both hands as the blood-red fireball she had seen once before emerged from his chest and settled onto both upturned hands. Though Dagon's Dragon Fire looked considerably smaller this time, likely because it had emerged from Taron's human form, it was still huge. She marveled how it didn't seem to burn the navy blue argyle sweater he was wearing at all on its way out of his body even though she could feel the immense heat radiating from it.

The collective anticipation of the guards behind them once their king's Dragon Fire appeared was so thick in the air that it made her skin crawl. Briana had to fist her hands at her sides to keep from vigorously rubbing her arms. Despite that, even she watched with bated breath as Taron placed the undulating red ball of fire over the center of his brother's chest and then drew his hands back. It immediately began to sink into Dagon's chest until its glow and heat disappeared completely.

For a couple of anxious seconds, his body remained deathly still, then Dagon gasped harshly, and his chest began to noticeably rise with breath. Briana unconsciously leaned closer in her excitement, but the silence stretched on without so much as an eyelash fluttering.

"It's done," Taron abruptly announced, making her jump.

"What do you mean 'it's done'?" she demanded. "He's still unconscious!"

He nodded. "And he'll continue to sleep for at least another day. Remember, he's been in a period of Soul Sleep for hundreds of years. From what the guards have told me, it seems there's a time discrepancy between this world and yours, so he's been asleep decades longer than the two hundred years of my exile. It's a bit like being in a deep coma for many years and then slowly awakening after all the trauma finally heals. The re-merging of the Dragon Fire with Dagon's body is a tedious process."

"Makes sense. So, what do we do now?"

"*You* are going to sit on the edge of this bed and rest while I go talk to the captain of the royal guard. You look a breath away from collapsing in exhaustion." He touched a hand to her cheek, making her wince as her abused skin still felt as sensitive as a day-old sunburn. "I know this day has been one big jumble of stress and confusion for you, so if you'll just bear with me for a moment longer while I get a better grasp of our current situation, we can then figure out how best to move forward."

He tapped the pocket of her jeans where the outline of the key was visible and then flashed her a meaningful look. She nodded curtly. Maybe he had been paying a lot closer attention to her earlier than she had thought.

Even after Taron and a guard with a sharp, almost angry expression whom Briana assumed was the afore-mentioned captain began an animated discussion in the guttural language of before while the rest of the guards resumed their guard duties with grim expressions, she felt the occasional eyes trying to bore holes into the back of her head. She did her best not to show just how much it bothered her by relaxing her shoulders and not turning to look at them at all while concentrating her gaze solely on Dagon's peacefully sleeping face.

She was more relieved than she cared to admit to herself that Taron showed no desire to abandon her at all now that she had fulfilled her role. She wondered what the other dragon-shifters thought of her, especially when they could probably smell her *Ansi* heritage. Would that make them suspicious of her intentions? Her loyalties?

Her eyes slanted briefly over to the door that was now closed. She wondered if Cabak realized that Taron had made it back home. What was the huge bastard doing now? More importantly, who was the witch that had sent the stone dragon to her world, and was that witch also hiding within Briana's world, waiting for Cabak to succeed in capturing Taron or building a portal back to Elysia even as she sat watching the dragon king?

Briana felt an invisible hand squeeze her heart painfully when she thought about Carol. She believed Taron's assurances that Harold Brown had protected Carol from harm, but her friend no doubt was frantic with worry. She had likely called the police. If only she would've had the chance to let the older woman know that she was okay, that Taron had saved her life by stealing her away from the shop.

Just what kind of hornet's nest would an investigation into a wealthy foreigner like Taron Hildebrand knock over, especially when they inevitably find that the man, himself, had also seemingly vanished off the face of the earth? What if she never managed to find her way home, dragon key or no dragon key? Carol would likely go to her grave thinking Briana had been murdered by Taron. And Mr. Brown? What had become of *him*?

By the time Taron returned to her side, Briana had worked her emotions up into an anxious knot.

"It's just as you said," Taron said as he sat down on the bed next to her. "About two years ago, the *Ansi* abandoned the stone dragons and barricaded themselves behind a magical shield cast around a single city near the royal palace. The stone dragons were just beginning to gain ground against the firedrakes protecting this tower when they were abandoned without warning or explanation both here and at the siege of the royal palace. The fact that neither this tower nor the royal palace has fallen under the control of the stone dragons is great news. I have always feared that I would return to a world that I no longer recognized."

"Two years ago—that's when you said Cabak first appeared in my world," Briana said.

Taron grimaced. "Yes, a coincidence that can't be ignored, and a cause for great concern. The flare of magic that brought us here wouldn't have gone unnoticed by the *Ansi*. A hole was opened in the fabric of this world by the power of the dragon key. They would recognize the magic's—flavor, for lack of a better word, and very likely guess that the true king will soon awaken from his Soul Sleep."

"Then, the *Ansi* really are after the Northern Dragon Throne, too," Briana cut in, feeling her mouth go dry at the thought of the type of offensive power a group of people who had the unfathomable knowledge to open portals between worlds might wield, "after your brother's body."

"Yes. The same laws dealing with a succession of the throne the stone dragons have been trying to exploit apply to the *Ansi*, as well. The ancient protection spells the *Ansi* of old placed on this tower have so far managed to keep the current *Ansi* from breaching them even with a portal, but according to Captain Rizall, ever since the *Ansi* defected from the stone dragons' side, they've redoubled their efforts in breaching the barrier. Several weaknesses have already been detected and no way to patch them. We can't risk waiting for Dagon to awaken here. We'll have to smuggle him out right under everyone's noses, somehow."

He lowered his gaze down to her pocket. His expression was suddenly unreadable.

"We also absolutely cannot allow the *Ansi* to learn of the existence of the dragon key. It's a magical item from another world that has no business wreaking havoc in this world. Thus, we must remove it from the equation, entirely."

Briana sucked in a sharp breath. "You mean, try to

use it on this room's door to open the way back to my world. What if Cabak destroyed the door on the other end or transformed back into his human form and is picking through the rubble as we speak? Plus, I might only have one shot at this to go back home. It might be safer for me to try it on a different door."

Out of the corner of her eye, she saw a few of the royal guardsmen stiffen when she mentioned Cabak and realized that even though they likely couldn't understand English, they were still listening very carefully to her conversation with their prince and would recognize the stone dragon's name.

Taron frowned. "You're right, and consulting Beatrice's book is out of the question as it's currently either under a pile of rocks and debris or in Cabak's hands."

The last was said with a scowl of disgust, and Briana seconded the feeling. Whether she made it back home or not, it seemed most of Beatrice Hildebrand's story would forever remain a mystery. The thought made her want to punch something.

Still frowning, Taron turned and asked Captain Rizall a question. Nodding at the other's short answer, he said, "Only my brother currently sleeps within the tower. We can go to the chamber one floor down and try that door."

Briana's heart sped up. Would that work? If she used

a different door, would she end up somewhere familiar, or like Taron, in a stranger's house in some remote corner of the globe like Iceland or Tasmania? She swallowed nervously. If she wanted to go home, then she had to try the key at some point. Waiting was just stupid.

She stared into Taron's sunset-colored eyes. Had it really only been a few hours ago that she had found them unnerving? Now she just thought them beautiful. She felt her chest tighten at the thought of never seeing this incredible man, this dragon-shifter, ever again.

Smiling to keep her sudden turmoil from showing, Briana nodded. "Okay. Let's try it."

CHAPTER ELEVEN

*T*he fact that Taron chose to guide her by the hand down the spiral staircase to the room below made Briana feel their impending separation more keenly. She was beginning to wish that she had never gotten to know the man within the scary dragon, though she couldn't really regret the hour they spent just chatting like friends while he flew her to England gripped within a dragon's hand.

The flickering shadows cast by the flames from the wall sconces made the whole scene surreal and dream-like. Once back home, how long would it be before she started to believe that the entire day's adventure never happened at all? At the very least, she could never tell anyone that Taron was really a dragon-shifter prince from another world, not if she didn't want everyone to wonder about her mental health for the rest of her life. Not even Carol.

Briana would've liked to have a more private goodbye with Taron, but once Taron had spoken with the guard captain about their intentions, Rizall had immediately barked a few commands to the nearest guardsmen, four of which proceeded to follow them out of the room.

She really couldn't blame them. The prince they had thought captured and lost forever had suddenly, miraculously, appeared safe and sound right before their eyes at a time when they needed him the most. Like hell they were going to let anything else happen to them while under their watch.

"What if I unlock the door and some weird alien landscape is on the other side?" Briana fretted as they stopped in front of the targeted door. A couple of the guards moved silently past them to take up positions a few steps down while the other two remained on the steps above them. "If the key disappears once I open the door? Do you think there's a single *Ansi* left in this world that would be willing to help me get back home?"

Taron released her hand and then reached up to gently cup her face with both. His hands always felt warmer than a human's, and they felt very soothing despite the "sunburn." His eyes were so beautiful, bright even in the gloom and seemingly swirling with real flames as he stared down at her so intently.

That his hair and parts of his face were still dusted with pulverized debris from his crumbling castle only made that moment seem more real. She wanted to seal it forever in her memory.

"Whatever happens, I'll do right by you. I promise."

As she offered him a tremulous smile, Taron's head suddenly swooped down, and Briana gasped when she felt the press of a pair of firm lips against her own that were searing in more ways than temperature. An equally scorching tongue lapped at her bottom lip teasingly before plunging aggressively into her mouth. A moan of surprise burst from her throat as she felt his slick tongue slide sensually against her own once, twice, and again. However, before she could get over her shock enough to really reciprocate, he pulled away.

Taron licked his lips, which then stretched into a grin of pure satisfaction. "I have wanted to taste those plump lips from the moment I first saw them lift up into a smile, and I was right. Your smile does taste incredibly sweet."

"You *had* to do that," Briana scolded, her voice sounding embarrassingly breathless. "You've just made it harder for me to leave."

Although the grin never left his lips, his tone was

utterly serious as Taron replied, "I know, and I'm sorry. But I would have deeply regretted it if I hadn't kissed you at least once."

Briana couldn't help it. Even though they had an audience, she surged up onto her tiptoes and planted a brief, but hard kiss onto that grin. Then she lowered her heels to the ground and wrapped her arms tightly around his waist in a firm hug.

"I'm really going to miss you, you big lizard," she mumbled against his sweater.

He chuckled as he hugged her just as tightly. "And I'm going to miss hearing you call me that almost as much as I'm going to miss you. Thank you for bringing me home. Now, let's get you back to yours."

Reluctantly, Briana pulled away from his warmth. She forced herself to smile up at him, wanting to leave him with at least that much even though she knew that the rest of her likely looked a mess.

"Thanks for the adventure."

Afraid that she would break down in tears if she said anything else, she turned towards the door and reached into her pocket for the dragon key. Although not as cold as it had been right after she had pulled it from the last keyhole, it was still chilly enough to make her fingers ache. Appearing as brittle as thin glass, she was surprised that the two teeth hadn't broken off after being shoved into her pocket a few times. Maybe it really was indestructible.

Before she could change her mind, Briana started to thrust the key into the lock when a blast from below knocked her onto her knees. The key slipped from her fingers and bounced precariously down a few of the steps. A split-second later, a flash of cobalt blue light rose up the stairwell from below, and one of the royal guardsmen flew past them at neck-breaking speed and crashed into the wall at the curve up ahead.

Briana didn't need to be told to know that what she had just witnessed was a magical offensive spell in action. The whole air seemed charged with energy as she instantly scrambled after the fallen key on her hands and knees down the stairs past Taron's legs, her hand barely having enough time to close around it before she was yanked up by the back of her sweater.

For the second time that day, Briana found herself hanging over Taron's shoulder as he raced up the stairs and around the fallen guardsman that was surprisingly struggling back onto his feet while the two guards above stayed behind to likely stand their ground against the threat coming from below.

More guards were coming out of Dagon's room by the time Taron reached the landing. It was almost comical the way they shoved him into the room with

Briana, herself, swinging precariously on his shoulder as he was jostled around like a pinball. Then Briana heard Captain Rizall shouting a bunch of incomprehensible words followed by Taron's slightly deeper voice. The only word she understood was *Ansi*, but it didn't take a genius to figure out that at least one of those weak spots in the magical barrier around the tower Taron had told her about had finally been breached by the witches.

Then Briana suddenly found herself on her feet again.

"Looks as though you won't be rid of me just yet," Taron said apologetically. "The tower has fallen. It's only a matter of time before the *Ansi* breach the barrier around this room. While the rest of the royal army runs interference and provides cover, I'm going to attempt to fly Dagon and you out of here. With any luck, we'll make it to one of the towns near the palace still under firedrake control. It's going to take a bit more cunning and effort to get Dagon back into the palace past the stone dragon's blockade currently barring the way."

"What can I do to help?" Briana asked as she followed him to the bed while stuffing the dragon key back into the front pocket of her jeans for the umpteenth time.

"After we break through that boarded up window, I need you to sit on that window sill and hold Dagon's body against you while I jump through and shift into my dragon form outside. The Fates willing, I'll then grab both of you in one fell swoop."

She nodded calmly even though her heart was beginning to race with rising fear and made her way over to the window to stand beside several of the guards. To find herself held within the talons of a dragon in the middle of what would probably be a dragon aerial battle full of fire, boulders, claw-to-claw combat, and God-only-knew what else would be beyond terrifying. Never mind falling to her death, she could end her life gruesomely in the jaws of an enemy dragon.

Taron picked up his sleeping brother as easily as though he were no heavier than a feather and carried him over to her. He nodded to the guardsmen and the two closest to the window instantly kicked at the boards covering it until they splintered. Then one by one, the guards stepped onto the wide sill and jumped out until only Taron and Briana remained in the room amidst a soundtrack of shouts, crashes, and growls down below and the roars of both dragons and shooting streams of fire outside the tower.

"Climb onto the sill and sit with your legs dangling over the edge," Taron instructed. "Once I arrange Dagon beside you, I need you to wrap your arms around his chest tightly and wait for m—"

The door behind them abruptly exploded, cutting

him off mid-word as they were bombarded by the flying remains of the door. Briana instinctually raised her arms to protect her face.

What the hell, again?

Through the cloud of dust in front of the gaping hole where the door used to be, she saw three figures standing, their hands glowing with blue fire. Briana was suddenly standing in front of the two brothers before she realized that she was going to move. She had only a split-second to wonder what the hell she was doing before the blast of blue power hit her squarely in the chest.

CHAPTER TWELVE

For the space of a heartbeat, the entire world turned blue as the force of the *Ansi's* attack shoved Briana back a couple of steps, effectively knocking the breath from her, but through sheer force of will, she remained standing as the blue power dissipated around her.

I'm alive...

"Briana!" Taron shouted anxiously behind her.

She could only shake her head as she gasped for the breath she had lost, confused about what had just happened. She had expected to see a huge, gaping hole in her chest similar to what used to be this room's doorway, but not even her sweater was damaged. Had that witch only fired the magical equivalent of a warning shot?

Her question was immediately answered by the second ball of blue power that struck her almost in the same area as the first. However, just like the first hit, the power appeared to dissipate on contact as she toppled backward against both Taron and Dagon.

A flurry of words was shouted at them from the *Ansi* in what sounded like a surprised tone, and this time, Briana saw the blue ball of power form in the hands of the man to the right of the woman who had cast the other two attacks at her. However, as she stiffened in preparation for the blast, Briana suddenly found her arms full of an unconscious, super-heavy dragon-shifter that caused them both to crumble to the ground. The *Ansi* then found themselves at the mercy of a snarling, slightly transformed Taron in full rage mode as the firedrake charged them, a stream of fire shooting from his mouth.

Unprepared for the sudden onslaught, only one of the *Ansi* managed to cast a protective shield around themselves as the fire roared over them. The other two screamed when their bodies lit up like a torch with orange-red flames. Taron slammed into the magical shield of the unscathed woman and bounced off hard, landing in an awkward crouch only a foot in front of Dagon and her.

Briana could see the nearly invisible ripples in the air

like a heat wave shimmering over the asphalt of a street in the distance as the magical barrier extended to cover the witch's comrades while the witch frantically began blasting them with power in an effort to put out the flames. The smell of burning flesh reached Briana's nostrils, making her gag.

"Now! While they're distracted!" Taron hissed urgently, pushing Briana towards the window with a clawed hand as he started to drag his brother to the window, as well.

Briana managed to get on her feet in record time and stumbled towards the window. She climbed onto the sill and sat on the edge. Taron set Dagon down next to her and allowed his brother to sag into her waiting arms before diving out of the window.

Knowing he would be all right, Briana turned her head to keep an eye on the *Ansi*. The uninjured one had managed to put out the fire on the other two and was currently on her knees frantically casting a spell over the still-writhing and smoking bodies, the witch's hands glowing a blinding white.

Two more probable *Ansi* appeared through the ruined door just as the scene was cut off by a large, red-scaled dragon hand that closed around both her and Dagon. Briana found herself once again uncomfortably squeezed within the fist of a dragon as well as pressed closely against the body of a virtual stranger.

Then the sight of two monstrously huge dragons filled her vision, one red and the other blue and as different as night and day in body types and the structures of their wings, and the discomfort of being pressed up so intimately against Dagon suddenly didn't matter at all. The dragons were in a death-hold, jaws clamped onto each other's neck, and feet with curved, wicked-looking talons clawed at the scales of exposed bellies.

It was both a relief and a cause for anxiety when Taron cupped his other hand over their heads for protection, plunging her into darkness. The next thirty or so minutes were a terror-fueled nightmare of roars, Taron spitting fire at enemies that made Briana feel as though she were being roasted, and a chaotic pattern of stomach-wrenching drops, rolls, and rapid rises until her head was a pounding, dizzy mess.

Through it all, Briana kept expecting one of the stone dragons to break through the dragons protecting Taron and ram into them hard, worried that her fragile human body couldn't survive that kind of blunt force impact even if it weren't a direct hit, but that brutal hit never came. It made her paranoid. She couldn't believe that they were actually going to escape this madness relatively unscathed.

In a way, what helped keep her calm was Dagon's steady breaths that rippled across her hair on the top of her head where his chin rested while he slept. She found if she focused on those soft breaths and not on the cacophony of madness around them, it helped keep her thoughts from spiraling into a panic.

A few minutes later, Taron's flight pattern became more stable, and the thuds, roars, and spewing flames of the dragon battle began to sound more distant. She hadn't dared tried to speak to Taron earlier for fear of distracting him at a crucial moment and wasn't sure if she should attempt to now even though she was dying to know what was going on.

Luckily, Taron took the decision from her by suddenly announcing, "We're finally clear."

Briana closed her eyes and heaved a huge sigh of relief. "Where are we now?"

"Taking the long way around again, unfortunately," he replied gruffly. "I had hoped at least one of the royal guardsmen would have been able to break away along with us. However, with the unexpected addition of the *Ansi* into the fray, it was all that our forces could do to create a hole within the stone dragons' attack formation and keep all of them from giving chase for the few minutes I needed to disappear from their line-of-sight. At least the *Ansi* cannot give us any trouble while we're in flight and hidden behind the clouds, but no doubt they will be ready for us at any number of places on the ground."

"Does that mean our original destination is a no-go?"

"Yes, but the secondary site will work just as well for our plans."

"So why do you sound so hesitant?" she demanded, hoping he wouldn't try to weasel his way out of telling her if it was something bad.

"It's for no reason as dire as I'm sure you're imaging." She could hear the smile in his voice. "We cannot fly directly to the secondary site. As it's a covert camp where a small battalion has been silently spying on the movements of the stone dragons' blockade of the royal palace, it's too near the enemy to fly in safely. It will require a considerable hike through a forest to reach it —at least the rest of the day. Naturally, I can't be in my dragon form."

"I can make it if that's what you're worried about," she said firmly. "I've run a couple of marathons within the last year, so as long as there aren't any mountains to scale and you don't plan to sprint the whole way, my stamina shouldn't be a problem at all."

"I was more concerned about the time being on foot will unavoidably waste, never mind any discrepancies in our stamina. I can easily carry both Dagon and you if I must. No, the problem lies with the fact that both the *Ansi* and the stone dragons will have the time to scour the globe for us via both flight and portal. We could very likely run into a dozen of either group within the forest, or if they are feeling desperate enough, they could choose to unleash their endgame. If the royal palace falls, then the only way to reclaim it is through my brother fighting the usurper-king in a fight to the death. It's a position I never want my brother to find himself in, no matter his strength."

"I just wish there was more I could do to help," Briana lamented in frustration.

"You have helped me more than you realize, I think," he chided. "Isn't it enough that you stopped that *Ansi's* magical attack not once, but *twice?*"

"Those were just warning shots, weren't they?" Briana asked in confusion. "I didn't do anything at all."

"That first attack had enough power to easily knock me unconscious," Taron said. "The fact that your body absorbed the magic on impact just proves the truth of your heritage even if my nose didn't."

"What do you mean?"

"*Ansi* magic is useless when used against another of the Blood. Their bodies naturally absorb it, and it seems even someone whose *Ansi* blood has been thinned considerably over several generations retains that one ability, even if you can't cast any spells."

"Great. My superpower is 'super absorption,' " Briana said dryly. "It figures I would end up with one of the lame ones."

Taron's laugh reverberated pleasantly over her skin. "I think 'Absorption Girl' sounds kind of endearing."

Briana snorted. "Yeah, as endearing as a tampon."

She swore he laughed for a good ten minutes.

It was a happy memory she held in her mind like an anchor after they had been hiking through what Briana was beginning to believe was an endless forest for a little over six hours. It was sweltering and humid, and it hadn't been long before she was sweating so badly that the streams of sweat running down her face had long ago washed off most of the remaining dust from various building collapses and explosions from her face.

She had even removed her sweater, thankful for the thin tee she had worn underneath, and had given it to Taron to tie around his waist as a makeshift loincloth as his own clothes had been shredded during his last transformation. However, at this point, walking around in just her underwear was beginning to look more and more attractive.

Taron, that bastard, was dry as a bone, of course. Briana suspected he even felt invigorated from the heat, but she kept her snark to herself, determined not to complain once. She was, after all, from Texas and had endured much worse heat and humidity.

At least her misery kept her mind away from obsessing about the possibility of ambush, though with Taron's keen hearing, at least no one could sneak up on him from behind. Still, she found herself peering up at the sky worriedly more times than was really necessary, half-expecting something to spring down on them from the treetops or to dive-bomb them from the sky. They also talked very little, wanting to remain as quiet as possible.

When she wasn't watching for hidden enemies or a stream to quench their thirst, Briana passed the long hours as she quietly followed after the two dragon-shifters by studying all the flora and fauna. Taron's world had way too many humongous flying bugs larger than her hand for her peace of mind, but their "birds" were absolutely beautiful. Many bore feathers in dozens of shades of green, purple, and brown along with elaborate, leaf-like patterns that made them practically invisible once they had landed on a tree branch.

The trees, themselves, were more familiar, similar to her world's oak trees in both color and form, if not the height. The trees in this forest would have given

Redwoods a run for their money in the height department.

As she was squinting at a patch of white flowers growing at the base of a tree they were passing on the right, Briana suddenly found herself flying towards those flowers from a hard shove to her shoulder. She barely managed to get her hands out in front of her to prevent herself from face-planting, but she still landed hard enough to cause pain to shoot up from her right wrist.

"Get behind that tree!" Taron hissed just as the world around them seemed to explode in a flash of blue light.

Her heart instantly in her throat, Briana scrambled on hands and knees to the other side of the enormous tree without question and turned to press her back against it. Then before she could even look up, Dagon's sleeping body was shoved onto her lap. She instinctively grabbed the heavy body around the torso and struggled to move the dragon king to a better position that wasn't both crushing her and obstructing her field of vision.

An inhuman roar sounded from her right, making Briana flinch, but she couldn't see either Taron or the probable *Ansi* who were attacking. She clutched Dagon closer to her body, hardly daring to breathe much less move no matter how anxious she was to see what was happening. The already-scorching air heated up several degrees as Taron countered the *Ansi's* magic with blasts and streams of red-orange fire. A feminine shriek sounded followed by a wet, choking sound that suddenly made her glad she couldn't see the fighting at all. Even only partially shifted, she imagined Taron's dragon claws could do some pretty gruesome damage.

More explosions of blue, yellow, and green light forced Briana to shut her eyes periodically to shield herself from their painful brilliance. Just how many *Ansi* were attacking? She opened her eyes and then gasped sharply as a man stepped out from behind a nearby tree, his hands limned with blue tentacles of magic that were forming into an attack.

"Shit!" she spat as she frantically pulled herself from beneath Taron's brother.

Briana barely managed to turn and curl around the dragon-king's body protectively before she felt the *Ansi's* power slam into her back and explode outwards in a flash of harmless blue light. The force of the blast stunned her long enough for the *Ansi* to reach them and start to tug her off Dagon. She abruptly turned and slammed her palm into the man's nose as hard as she could. She had a split-second to see his shocked expression and his hands fly towards his nose protectively before fury flooded his eyes, and his entire body surged visibly with power.

Dammit, I didn't even make his nose bleed... Briana thought disgustedly just as he thrust his hands forward, and she was hit point-blank with another dagger of power.

This time her breath was knocked from her, but she managed to stay on her knees and keep from collapsing onto Dagon. Even as she gasped for breath, Briana turned her head to glare back at the *Ansi* defiantly. Gasping or not, if the bastard took another step, he would be in the perfect range for her to punch him hard in the balls. Taron had entrusted his brother to her, and dammit, she wasn't about to lose him without a fight!

However, the *Ansi* wasn't attacking but staring at her in something like bewilderment. His eyes then narrowed, and he barked a string of foreign words at her. She merely responded by climbing back to her feet without a word and taking a protective stance in front of Dagon's sleeping body, her eyes never once leaving the man before her.

Now looking just angry, the *Ansi* started to speak harshly again but was abruptly engulfed in a dense stream of flames mid-sentence. He didn't even have time to scream, his body instantly incinerated until only a blackened husk of ashes and bone were left where he had once stood.

"Briana! Are you hurt?" Taron all but growled as he rushed towards her from the right.

A shiver went down her spine as she took in his face and body covered in large, red scales, the blazing-orange dragon eyes, and the black-clawed hands reaching out for her, but luckily her mind was still frozen in shock of the death she had just witnessed to show him any of that instinctual fear.

"I'm—okay," she wheezed as he gently took her face into his hands, his eyes scrutinizing.

Taron frowned. "You don't sound it."

"The *Ansi* you just fried blasted me with his magic and knocked the wind out of me. That's all," Briana insisted.

"My Absorption Girl. Yes, he was so confused and distracted when he realized that you were *Ansi* that he didn't sense me coming," Taron said.

"No wonder he tried to talk to me," she said, trying not to smile at the nickname while they talked about such a grim subject. "He thought I was someone from this world."

"I killed the other five, so your true identity is safe for now." He lifted his gaze and stared out into the trees with narrowed eyes. "I don't sense or smell any others, but it won't be long before this hunting party is missed. Even if I bury what remains of all the bodies, I can't hide all the scorch marks on the trees and ground nor the residual magic of our battle. This area is no longer safe for my brethren. We must hurry."

Briana was immensely pleased that Taron didn't even offer to carry her along with his brother even though she knew he was still worried about the magical attacks she had absorbed. It showed confidence in her stamina and made her feel less like a burden to him at such a critical time.

For the next two hours, they trudged through the forest at a brisk pace. She was even more paranoid when it came to all the surrounding sounds, no longer worrying about huge mutant bugs suddenly flying out at them from the trees or alien predatory animals but more *Ansi* waiting silently in ambush.

It was with these anxious thoughts that Briana nearly jumped clear out of her skin when her left hand was suddenly grabbed.

"Stay close to me," Taron murmured, his eyes narrowed and staring ahead into the distance. "I can't smell him, but I saw someone wearing a uniform of our army perched high in one of the trees far ahead. I don't want them to mistake you for the enemy."

Briana gripped his hand more tightly and nodded, her heart in her throat.

Taron slowed their pace to a more casual stroll,

walking straight ahead as the path around the trees allowed. Her shoulders tensed as she started to see shadows emerge from within the trees ahead, ten in total. They stood silently and merely watched them as their strange trio approached. It was only when they were about a hundred yards away that they finally realized who it was that was approaching so boldly because the firedrakes, to a person, suddenly rushed them like a determined line of tackles.

Before Briana could take a step back in alarm, every soldier dropped to their knees and bowed their heads in prostration.

The centermost soldier, a woman with shortly cropped black hair that curled up around her ears, was the first to raise her head, a grin threatening to split her face in half. She then began talking very animatedly in Taron's language while every eye in the vicinity tried to stare a hole into the center of Briana's forehead. Their expressions weren't exactly hostile, but nor were they anything that could be called friendly. She tried to ignore her growing discomfort by focusing on the conversation going on no matter that she had no hope of understanding any of it.

Two men approached Taron, but he shook his head. He said a few words, and the soldiers bowed before backing off. She guessed that they probably tried to take

Dagon from Taron's shoulder. She could understand why he wouldn't want his brother to leave his sight just yet.

Then Taron abruptly squeezed her hand, and she looked at him questioningly.

"Their camp is only about a mile up ahead," he said. "The fallen *Ansi* we left behind won't likely be missed until tomorrow. Dagon will also likely not awaken until morning, at the very least, so it will give me a chance to learn what I can to better advise him, as well as us to eat and rest before we have to move the camp."

Briana sighed internally. Another mile…

"Come to think of it, I haven't eaten since breakfast," she replied. She saw some of the soldiers still staring at her from the corner of her eye. Even though she knew they couldn't understand English, Briana still lowered her voice as she asked, "Are they worried about you bringing someone who smells like an *Ansi* into their super-secret camp?"

Taron looked at her sideways. "I explained about the nature of our relationship. They won't give you any trouble."

Whatever he told them, she hoped he hadn't mentioned the dragon key. The last thing she needed was curious or bored soldiers wanting to test it out.

Not that there are any doors out here, she thought wryly

as she allowed Taron to tug her by the hand after three of the soldiers while the others moved to resume their posts.

Briana had a feeling that she wouldn't be seeing any doors for a long time. She was surprised to find that she really wasn't all that upset about the fact.

At least spending time with Taron was guaranteed to never be dull. The memory of the feeling of his lips pressing firmly against her own rose, unbidden, in her mind, and she felt her cheeks flush with something other than embarrassment.

No, not dull at all.

CHAPTER THIRTEEN

*W*hen Briana returned from the stream the spy camp used for bathing, she was surprised to find Taron sitting alone next to the cot where his brother lay still fast asleep. When she had left with a female soldier named Ylda whom Taron said had volunteered to show her the stream, the dragon prince had been surrounded by soldiers. She had assumed that they would be bringing Taron up to speed and planning for Dagon's eventual awakening all night, so she had been planning to slip into the tent as quietly and unobtrusively as possible and head towards the separated partition in the very back that was meant for her.

She was currently wearing the dark brown shirt and an extra pair of breeches that Ylda had given her. As the dragon-woman had been much taller, Briana was practically swimming in them, but they were dry, clean, and comfortable, and that's all she cared about.

In her right hand, she tightly clutched the dragon key. Although it still gave her the heebies to touch it, she hadn't wanted to leave it in the pocket of her jeans while she had bathed, and she knew that Taron didn't think it was a good idea to let it out of her sight. That's why, against her better judgment, after Ylda had left her alone, she had taken it into the stream with her while she had bathed. A good thing, too, as she had found her dirty clothes replaced with the ones she was currently wearing when she had emerged from the water.

Taron appeared to have bathed as well, his black hair shiny and slightly damp. He was wearing a uniform identical to the soldiers'. She wondered if someone had filled a tub with water for him while she was gone. You can't expect a prince to bathe in a stream like a common soldier, after all. The thought of him bathing alongside her in the stream made her suddenly tingle in places best forgotten if she wanted to have a conversation with him without blushing.

"I thought you would still be talking with everyone," Briana said as she moved to stand beside the stool Taron was sitting on.

"It seems things have been at a stalemate longer than I had supposed," Taron replied with a sigh. "There wasn't much more they could tell me that Captain Rizall hadn't already relayed. The blockade is ten thousand stone dragons strong, and we have about the same amount on the other side defending the palace. It will not be easy to smuggle Dagon into the palace past that living stone wall."

His eyes then focused on her, roving up and down her form with keen interest before the ends of his lips quirked up. "You look like a little girl playing dress-up in your mother's pajamas."

Briana crossed her arms over her chest and shrugged. "Better than the grimy and sweaty clothes I was wearing. Someone's probably burning them now as we speak."

He laughed. "Or studying them. I haven't seen your sweater since I removed it from my waist. It's not every day that someone from a different realm steps into this world. I daresay if my sweater hadn't been shredded during my shift, it would have disappeared as well."

She looked down at Dagon's face. "Has he stirred at all while I was off taking a bath?"

"His eyelids fluttered once, but you shouldn't be too concerned. It will likely be hours, yet."

Taron's eyes abruptly sharpened as he noticed the dragon key in her hand. "There is nothing in this camp that even resembles a door, much less a lock."

Briana blinked at him in surprise. "Oh, I know. I only have it out because these clothes don't have any pockets. I suppose if I can find a small chain or at least a piece of twine, then I could loop it around my neck—"

She gasped as Taron suddenly pulled her down by the waist until she was sitting a bit awkwardly on his lap. His sunset eyes brighter than usual, he raised a hand to her cheek and lightly ghosted his fingertips down the curve of her sensitive skin, making her shiver.

"It may be months, even years, before we make it back to the palace," he murmured, his eyes fixed on the movement of his fingers while she sat frozen, hardly daring to breathe, "before we find a way to end this civil war, but at the same time, this war may end tomorrow or the next day. While a life on the run full of war and fear is not the type of life I would wish for you, if all of that were to end soon, what would you say if I asked you not to use the key, to lock it away deep within the palace vaults and never think about it again?"

Taron leaned forward and brushed a soft kiss onto her slightly-parted lips. "To stay here, with me?"

Stay...

Completely blindsided, Briana could only stare back mutely with wide eyes, her mind stuck somewhere between the thought of staying in another world for the rest of her life and the rush of arousal that his kiss had awakened within her.

After a long moment of stunned silence on her part, Taron suddenly shook his head and pressed his forehead against hers. "You don't have to answer me right now. Or even tomorrow or the next day."

Then before she could blink, Taron's lips crashed down onto hers, swallowing her gasp. She felt his fingers thread through her hair as he gripped both sides of her head and pulled her more firmly against him. That hot tongue that had delighted her earlier slipped within, and she shuddered as it aggressively slid against her own, coaxing her to respond with a tentative, wet caress.

Briana melted against him as she closed her eyes and utterly surrendered herself to his aggressive kiss, her fingers gripping his shoulders so tightly that they began to ache. She decided to accept this moment for what it was and not worry about what it could be.

She felt him smile briefly against her mouth before he released her head and slowly ran his hands down her back and over her ass. He gave both firm globes a playful squeeze before his hands gripped them tightly, and he proceeded to stand up. Briana hastily wrapped her legs around his waist as she sensed him walk towards the back of the tent where her bedroll lay, all while continuing to devour her lips.

Her entire body felt hot, as though it had been ignited with his dragon flames by his lips and touch alone. She broke their kiss with a half-gasp, half-laugh when he tumbled them onto the thin roll, his hips easily parting and sliding between her legs with a single, aggressive thrust against her pelvis that had the moist center of her throbbing, aching for more of that delicious stimulation.

Between one blink and the next, Briana's top was sliding over her head, her arms automatically lifting as Taron removed it. After tossing it to the side, he then bent down and licked once across both lips with a gentle, teasing flick before moving to lick slowly and more insistently along her chin and down across the center of her neck, his hair tickling her over-sensitized skin as his tongue continued its wet, sensual exploration southward.

Taron slowed his caresses as he licked closer to the top of her right breast. Briana squirmed in anticipation, already feeling her nipples begin to peak and throb even before she felt that first teasing swipe of the tip of Taron's tongue across her nipple.

Briana sucked in a sharp breath when she felt his mouth suddenly latch onto that same nipple, and she threw her head back and arched up into the sensation, her fingers sliding into his hair and tugging him closer in encouragement. Her thighs squeezed against the sides of his chest, and she bucked her hips in reaction as Taron continued to lathe attention on that sensitive little pebble, causing her clit to rub briefly against the rough material of her breeches. She bucked again with a sigh, chasing after more of that sensation.

Her dragon prince chuckled before he gave her nipple one final nip and lifted himself off her body with the strength of his arms until he was no longer touching her.

"Taron!" Briana moaned, arching her back up and reaching her hands up to him, suddenly desperate to feel his warmth across the length of her, to experience that teasing friction again.

"Is this what you want?" he asked, his voice deepened with rising lust as he reached a hand down beneath the waistband of her breeches to her naked sex and began to lightly rub over that little button of nerves in slow circles with the roughened tips of his fingers.

She cried out and bucked her hips. "Yes! Your mouth —please—!"

Taron removed his hand and made short work of taking off the last of her clothing. He spread her thighs wider with his hands, and she gasped as she watched him lower his head between her legs. The feeling of his hotter-than-a-human's exhales on her moist center was indescribably erotic, making her throb more painfully with arousal until she almost couldn't stand it.

A cry was wrenched from her throat at the first lap of a skillful tongue, and Briana clutched at both his hair and the blankets of the bedroll as Taron teased wave after wave of pleasure from her sensitive bud until she was jerking her head wildly from side to side and screaming with it. When her orgasm came, her entire body seized with the release as pleasure like she had never experienced before flooded her entire body and made something in her mind stutter and stop. It seemed the intense spasms would go on forever as Taron continued to skillfully massage her clit with his tongue.

"No more, no more!" Briana begged, tugging at his hair as she writhed mindlessly and tried to buck her hips against the hand Taron had pressed firmly onto her lower abdomen to keep her from doing just that.

Either he took pity on her, or the sound of her begging shattered the last of his control because suddenly that hot, hot mouth was devouring her lips as though he was determined to suck the life out of her and his equally hot, silky-hard member was pressing insistently against her still-trembling passage.

One hard thrust and his cock entered her all the way

to the root. Her cry of pleasure/pain was swallowed greedily as her thighs gripped his hips tightly. Damn, but she nearly felt split in two! Even when he had stood naked before her after shifting outside his castle, she hadn't given his member more than that initial glance as she had been too busy being bashful about his sudden nudity. She was suddenly grateful that she hadn't snuck more than an accidental peek back then and hadn't peeked at all before he had used her sweater to cover up his naked crotch here in the forest or else she would have probably been too frightened to take the whole of him.

Taron kissed the tears beginning to leak from the corners of her eyes as instead of pounding her into the ground as she had expected, his initial thrusts were slow and shallow, allowing her to get used to his sizeable girth. Only when she was able to finally relax and take him more easily did he begin to thrust powerfully and deeply, stroking nerves deep within her that no other had ever touched until her body was once again throbbing with building pleasure.

Briana relaxed her vise-like grip on his shoulders and slipped her fingers into his hair at the nape of his neck. She shivered when she realized that he was looking down at her with dragon eyes, his pupils thin and vertical along with irises the color of flames. It was somehow both sexy as hell and frightening at the same time.

"Taron," she breathed his name again, loving the way his eyes seemed to flash with an inner light whenever something she said or did elicited a strong emotion in him.

His hips sped up, his thrusts becoming more jarring and erratic as he alternated between soft, sweet kisses that were no more than a caress of lips and a sharing of air and sucking aggressively while tangling tongues, tittering on the brink of ecstasy. Briana was close to the edge, too, her passage squeezing his cock more tightly as her body stiffened that one second before everything within her exploded for the second time with one final, heavy thrust that nearly made her black out.

Then liquid fire abruptly flooded her passage, and Taron was biting at her neck with a groan and thrusting hard and deep once again as he climaxed. Briana clutched tightly at his shoulders and hung on for dear life.

When Taron's hips had finally stilled and Briana's body had stopped shaking so badly, he let out a sigh that was pure satisfaction and rolled them until she rested heavily on his chest. As her face pressed up against his heated skin that still smelled strongly of fresh ashes, she noticed that he was not sweating or breathing hard at all, the bastard.

She had never felt this emotionally and physically wrecked after sex, and she wasn't sure how to feel about that fact. No doubt this dragon-shifter had just ruined her for other men. Maybe that had been his intention all along, starting with that incredible kiss he had given her in the tower. Maybe he had hoped she would choose to stay with him even then. Not that she could blame her current dilemma entirely on him. After all, it did take two to tango.

Briana closed her eyes and buried her face into his chest with a frustrated sigh. "You don't play fair," she muttered just a bit resentfully.

What the hell was she supposed to do now?

Taron planted a kiss on the top of her head.

"No, I play for keeps."

CHAPTER FOURTEEN

*I*t wasn't until early the next morning, bleary-eyed and watching a gloriously naked Taron hunt around the space for his discarded clothes that Briana thought about the dragon key again and realized with a jolt of panic that she had no idea where it was at the moment. She remembered having it up until Taron had pulled her into his lap and kissed her. Had she dropped it then, or somewhere between Dagon's cot and her bedroll?

She sat up, blankets pooling forgotten around her waist and began looking around for her shirt. She vaguely remembered Taron tossing it aside after yanking it over her head…

"Briana?"

Taron had paused after pulling on his breeches, a

forest-green tunic in hand, and was now staring down at her with a hint of lust as well as concern. Realizing her boobs were on full display and her nipples erect, Briana quickly covered up with a blanket and shot him a half-hearted glare.

"Have you seen the dragon key?" she asked. "I dropped it somewhere around here last night."

He raised an eyebrow, before pointing to a space over on her right, his expression suddenly opaque. "It's right there next to your breeches."

She turned to look where he had pointed, and sure enough, the key was lying on the rug only a few inches away from where her head had just been resting. How in the hell had it gotten there? She slowly picked it up, half-convinced that it would be freezing to the touch just as it had been after she had used it to open the door into this world, but the glass-like substance was only cool.

A vision of the key growing legs and walking to the back of the tent in search of her while they had made love last night flashed within her mind's eye, and Briana shuddered. Just thinking about the bugged-out, color-less eyes of the dragon head possibly watching them have sex was the stuff of nightmares.

"This thing is really creeping me out right now."

"As I said last night, we can just lock it away if that's what you truly wish," he said carefully.

Briana sighed and clenched her hand around it. She said nothing, unsure what she *should* say, or even what she *wanted* to say.

A warm hand firmly lifted up her chin, making her start. She hadn't even heard him walk over. For a dragon, he sure moved around as silently as a cat.

Taron planted a gentle kiss on her lips that made her heart ache. "Hey, it's all right, remember? You'll soon learn that immortals are incredibly patient beings."

She flashed him a small smile. "You mean stubborn."

He laughed. "Yes, that, too." He dropped her brown shirt into her lap. "Get dressed. If you'll sit with my brother, then I'll go see about breakfast."

"Let's hope he waits to wake up until you're back. I can imagine the fun I would have trying to explain who I am when I can't speak your language or he, English."

Taron smirked. "One sniff and he'll know exactly who you are to me."

Briana looked up at him sharply. "On second thought, forget breakfast. I'll go wash in the stream again, instead."

"You're so adorable when you're shy," he said fondly as he finished dressing.

"I'm *not* shy," she grumbled. "You just have no shame."

His laughter at her expense followed him out of the tent, but she really couldn't fault him for teasing her so much when she made it so easy for him.

After dressing, washing her face using a pitcher of water and a metal basin, and finger-combing her hair, Briana searched around the tent for something that would allow her to create a makeshift necklace to hang the key around her neck. The only thing she could find was a black scrap of the same kind of linen-like material as her shirt and breeches and what she guessed was a small whittling knife. She settled down onto the stool beside Dagon's cot and set to work cutting the cloth into a strip narrow enough to twist to somewhat resemble a cord necklace.

By the time Taron returned with a plate full of an undeterminable type of meat and slices of a green-colored fruit, Briana had finished making her necklace. The key was currently tied to it like a charm and the necklace around her neck. The key rested against her chest, hidden beneath her shirt. Deciding that it was probably better not to ask about the meat, she accepted the food with thanks and without question.

"He hasn't so much as twitched the whole time I was watching him," Briana said as they ate.

"My father once had a Soul Sleep last a hundred and twenty years. It took him almost two days after his

Dragon Fire was given back to him for him to awaken. I know it's the human way to always be on the go, but in this matter, there really is nothing more to be done but to wait."

She nodded and then nearly dropped the piece of fruit she was holding when she realized that a pair of sunset-colored eyes that were not Taron's were now staring up at her. She started to say Taron's name, but he must have noticed that Dagon was awake at the same time because he suddenly leaned forward and began talking to the older dragon-shifter in his language a-mile-a-minute.

Through that whole discourse, Dagon kept looking between Taron and her with an unreadable expression, speaking only a few phrases here and there that had the intonations of questions before he finally nodded and rose from the cot into a sitting position. Briana hastily scooted her stool over so Dagon could swing his legs over the side if he so chose.

Even though he was Taron's brother, this was the *king* of the dragon-shifters. Forget not being able to talk with him, she had no idea how she was supposed to act around him. Was it rude to look him directly in the eyes? Was it all right to offer her hand to him for a shake?

However, Dagon saved her from working herself up

into an anxiety attack by nodding towards her and saying his own name followed by a few words she didn't know. She immediately bowed her head and replied, "Briana Wright. It's nice to meet you, too." She then turned to Taron and added, "Can you tell him that last part for me?"

He grinned. "Of course. I definitely need to start teaching you Draknar sooner rather than later."

She agreed. She was tired of feeling so awkward around everyone. The thought brought her up short. Her easy acceptance of language lessons was as though she already expected to be in this world for some time. Was it her imagination or did the dragon key suddenly feel a little bit colder against her skin?

Taron abruptly took her hand and urged her to stand. "Come on. Now that my brother's awake and I've told him what has happened to our father, me, and this kingdom, we need to go meet with the soldiers of this camp."

Briana marveled at how calm and collected Dagon was after being told that his father had been assassinated and the kingdom plunged into a civil war while he had been in his Soul Sleep. She wondered how long he had meant to sleep in the first place. True that three hundred years was probably a drop in the ocean in the whole scheme of things, but three hundred years was three hundred years. A lot could happen in that time even for an immortal. In this instance, a prince had become a king in the worst possible way.

The next few hours were a flurry of conversations and activity that Briana mostly sat clueless through as she was loathed to ask Taron anything while he was so obviously up to his eyeballs in war plans with his brother. That's why it took her a moment to sense the rising tension in the group, but once she had, it wasn't hard to guess its source. The more she watched Taron and Dagon speak with each other, the harder and harder their expressions became and the blanker the surrounding soldiers' faces became until Briana started to worry that they were about to come to blows.

Feeling useless, she could only watch silently from a stool next to Taron and hope she wasn't going to have to get between two snarling dragon-shifters before long. Then Taron spat something that sounded like an expletive and straightened up from where he had been leaning close enough to his brother to literally butt heads.

It seemed Dagon had won the battle, whatever that battle was. Even so, the dragon king didn't look triumphant at all. If she had to say, Dagon just looked sad as he regarded Taron's angry face.

Briana hesitantly touched Taron's hand, wanting to

comfort him but not sure what was wrong, what he needed.

Taron turned to her and shook his head. "There's no need for you to fret," he said quietly. "My brave but foolish brother just made a decision that I've been trying to save him from making."

Her eyes slanted over to Dagon, who was watching them out of the corner of his eye while listening to one of the ranking soldiers, and then back to Taron's grim face. "What can I do to help?" she demanded.

He reached over beneath the table and linked their fingers together. "Just stay by my side," he replied gruffly. "Stay by my side while we all watch my brother challenge Jathar of the House of Blue Stone to a fight to the death."

CHAPTER FIFTEEN

*B*riana had expected the group of royal messengers Dagon had sent into the midst of the stone dragon's blockade to parlay with the enemy to not return for at least a day. However, an hour after they had first departed, their camp looked like a colony of ants scrambling around after a firecracker had been set off among them. The stone dragons had accepted the dragon king's challenge.

One-by-one, the soldiers had shifted into their fire-drake forms until a magnificent dragon army stood among the trees like a surreal fantasy painting.

The last to shift were Taron and Dagon. From his tone as they talked animatedly, she got the sense that her lover had tried one last time to talk his stubborn brother out of the fight, to no avail. Finally, Taron just sighed and leaned over to embrace his brother fiercely before stepping away to allow Dagon to shift.

He then walked over to Briana and reached over to tug softly at the cloth necklace around her neck. "If the worst should happen, the new king will demand my head in the name of peace. For the sake of my people, it's something I will not attempt to avoid. I have already instructed Ylda to make certain you are given an opportunity to use this key."

Briana flashed him a stricken look. "This is why I *hate* monarchies," she said thickly. "All these stupid rules just for the sake to retain power."

Taron bent down and kissed her soothingly on the forehead. "I know, but sometimes those same rules in the right hands can usher in a longstanding peace."

A thunderous roar sounded behind them as over a hundred red and black dragons flapped their wings and took to the sky.

"Looks as if that's my cue to shift."

Like his brother, Taron embraced her firmly. However, before he released her, his lips crashed down onto her own and kissed her hard and desperate as though it would be their last.

Briana felt as if she were tearing off a scab from a wound when he finally pulled away and she had to release his tunic from her grip. She struggled not to cry as he stepped a good distance away from her so he could shift.

The dragon key felt like a cold, dead weight against the skin of her chest.

For perhaps the last time, she watched Taron transform into a magnificent firedrake. She was so intent on watching his enormous wings unfurl to their maximum width that she failed to notice the person behind her until a pair of arms roughly grabbed her around the torso. The last thing she saw before everything went black was Taron's suddenly blazing dragon eyes as he opened his mouth to roar in utter fury.

For a few terrifying seconds, Briana couldn't breathe within that total darkness. Then the feeling of her neck being tightly squeezed by an invisible hand abruptly eased, and she gasped sharply, her lungs filling with a burst of warm air.

"Don't struggle," an unknown voice echoed within her head, making her violently flinch.

Weird voices whispering in her head—yep, she had definitely just been kidnapped by witches at the worst possible time. They must have been either ballsy or desperate to snatch her literally right from under Taron's nose. She couldn't tell if it had been a man or woman that had spoken which unnerved her just as much as the thought that someone had the ability to directly access her brain at will.

Her surroundings were still hidden in total darkness, but now Briana could sense others moving around in front of her, making the hairs on her arms stand on end. The scent of dust and the lack of a moving breeze told her that she was likely now within a dwelling of some sort. These witches could teleport, too?

It took every ounce of her control not to struggle against the thick arms that still imprisoned her body, but the logical part of her brain knew that struggling now when she had no idea where she was would get her nowhere. She had bigger things to worry about right now such as the dragon key hanging beneath her shirt that she absolutely had to keep them from finding if she didn't want to see her chances of getting back to her world fall to zero.

It was only then, with that anxious thought that Briana realized that she couldn't feel the smooth coolness of the key at all even though her captor's forearm should have been pressing it firmly into her chest. Shit, had it fallen off her makeshift necklace when the bastard had grabbed her?

No, no, don't panic. Don't panic. Not having the key is a good thing. Once you escape, you and Taron can go back to the firedrakes' camp and look for it. No big deal...

"What do you want from me?" Briana demanded stiffly.

"*Speak to me within your mind,*" the *Ansi* said. "*We can't understand your tongue otherwise.*"

Staying silent would get her nowhere, so with a massive dose of apprehension, Briana repeated her question in her mind, half-afraid that by doing so she would be inadvertently opening her mind up even more to these witches. Why, why didn't she ask Taron more questions about the *Ansi*?

"*We don't need you,*" the sexless voice in her head replied. "*You are weak in the Blood and would only add weakness to your people in a time when we must be at our strongest. We need what you have brought back into Elysia, an artifact of limitless power that your ancient, traitorous ancestor stole from us when he fled with it to your world.*"

The dragon key.

Briana laughed mirthlessly. "*Then you're out of luck because I don't have it.*"

"*The Key of All Faces cannot be lost by its chosen wielder. Not until its true task is done.*"

Key of All Faces? Wasn't it just her luck to get abducted twice for a damned magical key, but at least Taron had been after the key she'd actually had in her possession.

"You're barking up the wrong tree. I don't have or have never had the key you're looking for!"

"Nothing good will come from protecting our conquerors!" Briana could feel the *Ansi's* anger surge into her like a thundering river, making her flinch again. *"Only one of* Ansi *blood could have brought the exiled dragon prince, Astaron, back from the other world and* only *with the power of the Key of All Faces. I was there in the forest. I saw with my own eyes how that fire beast slaughtered my brethren while* you *protected King Dagon with your own body and walked away unscathed as only one of the Blood could!"*

Crap. No wonder they were able to find the fire-drakes' secret camp so quickly. Taron had missed at least one pair of hidden eyes in the forest.

"What do you mean conquerors?" Briana asked carefully.

She knew next to nothing about the *Ansi.* If she wanted to get out of this alive, she needed to keep them talking, to make it seem as though she might be sympathetic to their cause, to play the complete innocent if she could.

"Whatever those dragon-shifters have told you about us are complete lies," the *Ansi* said firmly. *"The dragons came tens of thousands of years ago to this world like an unstoppable plague and enslaved our ancient ancestors. Those creatures were not born of this world. They are usurpers! The*

firedrakes would have you think that the Ansi *have betrayed their trust by siding with the stone dragons in their civil war. I ask you this—how can we betray those whom we have never willingly sworn allegiance to in the first place? Those who have stolen our lands and destroyed our traditions to the point that many of them have been lost to even memory over the ages?"*

"*I haven't heard any of that,*" Briana admitted, though none of what the *Ansi* told her was as shocking as her captor had likely intended.

As a student of history, she knew very well that there wasn't a human civilization in the ancient past that *hadn't* conquered or tried to conquer their neighbors or even the known world. Why would it be any different for dragon-shifters and witches?

Albert Einstein had said it best: "So long as there are men, there will be wars."

What mattered to her the most was a person's intentions, and that's what she would hopefully learn here. The *Ansi* had apparently been trusted enough by the firedrakes to serve in positions that were close to the king, close enough that they were able to help the stone dragons assassinate Taron's father. They had also been the ones to cast the protection spells around the tower where the firedrakes stayed during their Soul Sleep, a time when they were at their most vulnerable. That kind of trust wasn't something given to another if that other was thought lesser.

"*Of course you haven't,*" the *Ansi* sneered. "*Astaron is known for his silver tongue. He has no doubt dazzled you with his true form and earned your sympathy with tales of the injustice of our actions. However, now that you know the truth of our injustice, it's not too late for you to undo the damage bringing the exiled prince back to Elysia has wrought. You can now be the savior of your people instead of our doom.*"

"*I told you—I don't have any key,*" Briana lied. "*It was lost in my world when the stone dragon, Cabak, in his dragon form crashed into the door we used to open the way into this world. I don't understand what you think I can do with it even if I did.*"

"*And I told you, the key* can't *be lost,*" the *Ansi* replied a bit impatiently. *It will eventually come back to you, and when it does, we'll be ready to act.*"

"*What can a key that only opens doors between worlds do for your cause?*" Briana asked again with a sinking feeling. Were the *Ansi* planning a freaking invasion of *her* world?

"*Not just a door,*" the *Ansi* said smugly. "*With your hand and the combined efforts of every* Ansi *within this city, we can create a portal to your world today that will swallow every firedrake and stone dragon during their barbaric fight for the throne.*"

"*Why should I help you do to my world what you've just lamented happened to yours?*" Briana asked incredulously.

"*Because it's the only way you will see your home again,*" the *Ansi* said matter-of-factly. "*Out of respect for our shared blood, we'll give you a few moments to yourself to consider everything you have learned here. Let's hope that when I return, the reluctance I sense in you now will have vanished. One way or another, we* will *have that key, and its face will show, not a dragon or an* Ansi, *but the face of your world.*"

With parting lines like that, you're not helping your cause at all, Briana thought sardonically as she was shoved down hard onto what felt like a wooden chair.

She was then bound tightly to the back of the chair with a thick, scratchy rope looped several times around her chest. Her wrists were also bound together, though thankfully, separately and not to the chair.

It was only when she heard a door open and shut followed by the distant sound of footsteps that Briana realized they really were going to leave her sitting there alone tied up in the dark. Being in the dark inadvertently made her think of the large insects and bugs she had seen during her trek through the forest with Taron, and with a shudder, she prayed to everything holy that there were none in the room with her. Huge bugs crawling up her legs when she couldn't even see them or scramble away were definitely her kryptonite in this screwed up scenario.

Although her hands and arms were bound, with a little wiggling, Briana was able to lift her hands high enough to pull her cloth necklace out from beneath her shirt with her thumbs. It confirmed what she already had suspected. The dragon key—or was it the Key of All Faces?—was gone.

The *Ansi* had seemed to imply that she could call the key to her at will. Was that true? Briana turned her head towards the direction of the door. Surely it wouldn't be that easy. Surely the *Ansi* wouldn't be stupid enough to leave her alone near a door with a lock, tied up or not. Yet… Her legs weren't bound. She was already screwed, so what would it hurt to examine the door just in case?

Damned if I'll allow the Ansi *to use me as a pawn, no matter their reasons!* she thought angrily.

Anyone who would threaten someone they knew was innocent with implied torture wasn't anyone she would ever help. The dragon-shifters may not be anywhere near guiltless in this whole mess, but Taron had never once intentionally hurt her. He also had never once tried to take the dragon key away from her once he had decided that he wanted her to stay with him here in Elysia. He had made it clear from the beginning that the choice to stay or remain was one hundred percent hers.

Briana carefully leaned forward as she slowly stood, the weight of the heavier-than-expected wooden chair tied to her back nearly tipping her to the ground. A startled curse slipped from her lips as her feet stumbled noisily on the wooden floor in a hasty attempt to rebalance herself, and she froze, suddenly afraid that someone would come in to check on her because there was no way her door was unguarded.

It was probably a full minute of silence before she could breathe again. She had to hurry. She had already wasted too many of the precious minutes her *Ansi* interrogator had given her to stew in what they likely thought was her own fear and the realization of their inevitable victory.

Still hunched over in an awkward position, Briana carefully shuffled towards the door as fast as she dared. Along the way, she thought hard about the dragon key, trying to will it to appear between her bound hands, but she didn't even feel a flutter against her skin.

Then without warning, the entire room shook amidst a deafening crash, and Briana was knocked onto her side, causing her to jab her thigh painfully on the edge of the chair's seat. The door crashed open just as she began struggling against her bindings, allowing a bright yellow glow from an unknown light source to cut through the darkness that made her squeeze her eyes shut against the unexpected onslaught.

She could hear several panicky voices shouting strings of incomprehensible words in the distance. What in the world had happened? Then a roar that made the very air tremble drowned out the shouts, and Briana could have cried. Whether it was Taron come to rescue her or not didn't matter. That a dragon or dragons had appeared to cause mayhem and destruction was the very distraction she needed for an escape.

That's why she stayed perfectly still while an *Ansi* man cut away at the bindings on her chair and allowed him to haul her up to her feet by her bound wrists without even a token fight. For added effect, Briana widened her eyes with an expression that she hoped telegraphed immense fear. The man didn't even try to talk to her as he jerked her by her wrists towards the door. Another boom sounded, this one much louder, and small pieces of rock and wood from the high ceilings began to rain onto their heads.

Briana had a brief glimpse of gray stone walls with sconces bright with a yellow illumination that could have come from something like a lightbulb or magic, she wasn't sure, before another crash sent her careening hard into the *Ansi*. By sheer will, she managed to keep her feet, but her captor had fallen to the ground.

A split-second was all it took for her to recognize her opportunity, and Briana turned to sprint down the corridor like the Devil, himself was after her. The dragon roars outside were almost deafening, but hearing them only seemed to lend more speed to her legs. Her first thought was to find a door that led outside or a window where she could get one of the dragons' attention, her next hit her like being doused in the face with a cooler full of ice water.

What if the dragons outside were stone dragons attacking this *Ansi* city out of retaliation for being abandoned and betrayed by their once-allies? She would be jumping from the frying pan right into one humongous fire that had nothing to do with firedrakes. She didn't want to think about what Taron would sacrifice for her life. No, she had to find somewhere to hide, somewhere with a window where she could make a more educated decision about her next move.

Footsteps pounded behind her, reminding her of the fallen man she had left behind. She had yet to run into anyone else, but no way would that remain true the deeper she ran within the building. She skidded around the corner and practically threw herself inside the first door she came upon that was ajar. She forced herself to close it gently, then searched in the near absolute darkness by touch alone for some way to lock or bolt it, but with horror, she realized that although her fingers had found what appeared to be a keyhole beneath a latch, she didn't have the key to lock it.

And no freaking dragon key to take me away from this madness, either!

Briana whipped around, her eyes squinting as she frantically searched the dark room. It was full of several shapes she could barely make out as barrels and large crates. A storage room. She was even more dismayed to find that the room also didn't have a window. Dammit, she would have settled for even a boarded up one at this point. If her *Ansi* pursuer found her now...!

She was so focused on trying to find something sturdy but not too heavy for her among the crates to move to barricade the door that she didn't realize what the sudden feeling of heaviness in her hands was at first until she felt it slide smoothly against her skin. Sucking in a sharp breath, Briana curled one of her hands around the object and felt the deceptively delicate teeth of a key.

CHAPTER SIXTEEN

*H*ad she been the crying type, Briana would have sobbed in relief at this sudden change in her fortune. She never thought she would be so glad to feel that cursed key in her hands again, and damned if she was going to let this opportunity go to waste!

She quickly turned and began to awkwardly feel around for a keyhole again, still unable to see hardly anything in the darkness. It took her a few more agonizing seconds for her fingers to slide across the small void. She then forced herself to carefully and slowly maneuver the key within her bound hands until she gripped the head securely between her right thumb and index finger while she listened hard to the chaotic sounds on the other side of the door as well as the crashes above.

It would be just her luck to be seconds away from escape only to have the ceiling come crashing down on her head.

It was when Briana finally managed to insert the dragon key into the keyhole that the door suddenly began to open.

"Shit!" she hissed and reflexively hit the door with her shoulder as hard as she could before it could open more than a crack.

Briana desperately twisted the key to the right, nearly choking on her rising panic as she forced herself to then tug on the latch to *open* the door with only one thought, a plea for the key to unlock a portal that would lead her to Taron and not open right into the hands of the *Ansi* that had started to open the door. Brilliant light flooded into the room as the door swung open, and she instantly shut her eyes with a cry of discomfort. In that split-second of instinctive hesitation, she half-expected to feel the hands of her pursuer angrily grab her shoulders, for the key to have failed, but nothing touched her.

A deafening dragon roar right above her had Briana's eyes instantly flying open. Squinting and half-blind in the sudden illumination, it took her a few tense moments to understand what she was looking at. The door had opened up to a cobblestone road with a row of crumbling stone buildings beneath the blazing sun about fifty feet across the way, the ruined stones smoldering heavily and the acrid scent of smoke thick in the air.

The area appeared empty of people, but she could hear the crackling of fire, booms, as well as people shouting or screaming in both terror and pain somewhere very close to her left. Was she still in the *Ansi* city she had been brought to? Had she screwed up her instructions somehow, and the dragon key had merely opened up a door that would allow her to come in contact with a dragon, any dragon? Maybe because Taron wasn't currently near a door? She had no freaking idea.

The fact that there was fire amidst the destruction pretty much sealed the deal that at least some of the dragons attacking were firedrakes. Even so, with the hellish scene she had stumbled into, should she even risk going outside to find out? In all the chaos, she could very easily be mistaken for an enemy by the firedrakes. She couldn't imagine a worst way to go out than death by fire.

Her gaze fell on the dragon key still sticking out of the keyhole. The smartest thing she could do right now was to shut the door and try to will the key to open up a portal back to her own world. It's what she *should* have done in the first place, and yet...yet...

The only thing I could think of was to get back to Taron.

Dammit. Not only would it be an asshole move to leave without at least warning the firedrakes about the *Ansi*'s ultimate plan for them, but the truth was she still wasn't sure if she wanted to go back home, to turn her back on the love that had started to bloom between her and Taron.

Feeling like the world's biggest idiot, Briana grabbed the dragon key and stepped outside just as a sudden gust of hot air swept over her from the right, sending her tumbling to the ground surrounded by a thick cloud of dirt. Coughing, she raised her head in enough time to see the tail-end of an enormous red and black dragon as it soared overhead, a stream of fire erupting from its maw that was directed towards a target she couldn't see to its left. She hadn't seen Taron in his shifted form nearly enough to recognize his dragon on sight, but a firedrake was a firedrake. Even if the dragon wasn't Taron, this was her best ticket out of the *Ansi* city.

After making sure that the dragon key was still clutched tightly within one fist, Briana pulled herself to her knees. She raised her bound hands, making them as visible as possible, and shouted, "Taron! It's Briana! I'm here! Taron!"

Please, please let it be Taron...

The dragon continued to fly farther away along its

current path of fiery destruction without so much as a head turn. Dammit, had he not heard her? Was she actually going to have to go out into the middle of the road beyond any hope of protection and wave her hands wildly in the air? She looked around nervously but wasn't comforted at all when it appeared as though her initial assessment of the area being empty was correct. This whole current nightmare started because she and Taron had missed the hidden *Ansi* watcher in the forest. One of the bastards could easily sneak up on her again and teleport her away before she could even blink.

Worse, though she could hear the thunderous flapping of the firedrake's wings, Briana could no longer see it in the sky. Maybe it would be best to get back into the building and wait for the dragon to come back around—

Briana shrieked as a red and black dragon abruptly landed only a few feet away from where she was still kneeling, its expression one of an apex beast in full murderous rage mode. Completely frozen in sudden terror, she didn't even have time to open her mouth to scream when the dragon lunged at her with one of its huge-ass claws. However, instead of the searing pain of being sliced to shreds, she was snatched up within the dragon's fist, and with two strong flaps of its wings, they were airborne.

"T-Taron?" Briana stuttered, on the verge of hyper-ventilating.

"It's all right now. I've got you," Taron's familiar dragon-voice growled above her as her view of the sky was cut off by his other hand forming the usual dome over her head to protect her from the air currents and other dangers.

Briana took a shuddering, relieved breath before she shouted, "You scared the shit out of me, you jerk! I wasn't sure if it was you that was attacking, and suddenly a huge, royally pissed off fire dragon with murder in his eyes is coming at me with claws longer than I am tall!"

"Sorry, sorry," he said, his voice still gruff with traces of his earlier rage. "I came alone as there was no time to recruit any of my brethren. I would've preferred a gentler rescue, of course, but the advantage of my surprise attack was beginning to wane. The *Ansi* had started to better organize their concerted attacks against me. They were seconds away from blasting me with an offensive spell that would have surely incapacitated me just as I snatched you."

"How in the world did you even find me so quickly? Get through the magical shield you told me the *Ansi* had cast around the city? You started blasting the hell out of everything before I tried to use the dragon key to escape, so that wasn't why."

"You used the dragon key?" Taron asked, sounding alarmed. "Did any of the *Ansi* see you do it?"

"No, but it wouldn't have mattered. They already knew I had it, though they called it the Key of All Faces. One of them saw our fight when we were ambushed in the forest and put two-and-two together when they saw me absorb a magical attack without damage. Apparently, the key originated here in Elysia and was stolen away to my world by my ancestor."

"And they want it back," he spat angrily.

"Desperately," Briana agreed, "but not for the reasons you're probably thinking. It's much worse. They were never on the stone dragons' side at all. They've just been using the stone dragons' bitterness about the throne to cause the very showdown that's happening now between your brother and Jathar. While I can't be sure if anything they told me is true, one of them laid their whole plan out for me as well as an extremely brief history between the *Ansi* and dragon-shifters as they saw it in hopes of swaying me over to their side."

"They told you that we are their conquerors," Taron interjected, sounding surprisingly matter-of-fact. "That part, at least, is true. There's no way to pretty up what was for both sides, a terrible war in our ancient past."

"They consider themselves enslaved," Briana said slowly.

"In the beginning, maybe that was true," Taron replied grimly. "However, I have never seen the *Ansi* treated as anything less than respected citizens of this kingdom during my lifetime. At least, until we were betrayed. I suppose some old wounds will never heal. You were right. They wish to retake the kingdom that was once theirs, alone, and what better way than to have us weaken ourselves tremendously in this civil war. With your key, they could accomplish this faster by exiling both Dagon and me, possibly even Jathar."

"Taron, they don't want the key just to exile royal dragon-shifters," Briana warned. "They want it to help them exile *all of you*. To *my* world."

"What!" Taron roared, making her wince at the unexpected decibels.

"They want it so much that they even insinuated they would torture me into compliance if I refused to use the key to help them. The only reason why I was able to get out of the building for you to find me was because they thought they would do me the 'kindness' of leaving me alone in the room where they had tied me to a chair to make up my mind about helping them willingly. What a joke."

"I would have found you, regardless," Taron said. "I

shared my essence with you. It's like a beacon that calls to me."

"I think it's best that I don't think too hard about what that actually means," Briana retorted. "We can talk about it later. Right now we both have bigger things to worry about. I realized while I was at the complete mercy of the *Ansi* that I know next to nothing about them, about their power. Is the dragon key or Key of All Faces or whatever one of their creations? Is that why they seem so confident that they can use it to shove all dragons into my world? Or is the key some sort of cosmic, magical artifact they merely found, and they're just deluding themselves about what they can do with it?"

"I know as much about the dragon key as I have told you, and all of it I learned while living in your world. I have never heard of a magical item called the Key of All Faces in either world. However, with the possibility of such catastrophic consequences, we must go forward as though the key you hold is, in fact, this Key of All Faces and that it *is* as powerful as the *Ansi* believe."

Briana's grip on the key tightened. She suddenly felt as though she held a ticking time bomb instead of something as innocuous as a key.

"What should we do?"

"For now, we go to watch the foolishness the *Ansi* have driven us to." The anger was back in Taron's voice.

"You know that's where and when the *Ansi* planned to open the portal that would exile everyone," Briana fretted. "They could still try to pull something. Maybe use their magic to do another snatch and grab of me and the key. I could feel them inside my head when they talked to me! For all I know, they could take over my mind, and there wouldn't be a damned thing I could do to protect myself from such an insane attack!"

"Don't worry. The *Ansi* have to be able to visually see their targeted destinations when teleporting, but more importantly, it's not magic they can do at a drop of a hat or magic that is taken lightly. Whether opening portals between worlds or teleporting to instantly shorten distances in this world, a terrible price must be paid each time, so they won't be so quick to use this method again."

"I can't even begin to fathom what kind of price would have to be paid to open a portal between worlds if their magic is based on some sort of give and take balance system."

"The price paid, my dear Briana, is the particularly painful death of slowly being dissolved alive from the outside-in, and not just any death. Two of the most skilled and powerful *Ansi*, their life-forces bound together as though they are a single life, are always required for such a spell. One to fuel it as the sacrifice, and one to weave the spell and still be living at the other end to carry out the task. Just as a dragon-shifter's immortality is fueled by their Dragon Fire, an *Ansi* can only draw from their own life-force to fuel their spells. The power required to teleport, roundtrip, is always more than the life-force of even the most exceptional witch, so you understand, right? The spell-caster is killing one of their brethren in one of the most horrific ways by their own hand. The price can't be avoided since adding more people to the spell is useless as it would only increase the amount of energy needed to reach the destination and as a consequence, the amount of dead bodies at the other end. As we speak, the body of an *Ansi* lies rotting in the forest where you last stood."

"Price or no price, if they're desperate enough..."

"But are they?" he countered. "They are bitter and discontent about what they lost in the past, yes, and have every right to be. However, I can say with a clear conscience that the *Ansi* have also thrived under dragon rule. Maybe the instigating factor of all of this was something as simple as a charismatic leader who rose up and stirred up those old hurts just as Jathar did for the stone dragons, and their initial intentions were indeed to swoop in and steal the Northern Dragon Throne while we were too distracted with fighting the stone dragons."

Briana stilled. "Then the firedrake prince they had exiled along with the Sleeping dragon king's Dragon Fire managed to find his way back home from the very world where they believed the Key of All Faces had been stolen to, accompanied by a woman with *Ansi* blood from the bloodline of that ancient thief."

"Don't beat yourself up about it. Given that the *Ansi* told you that they have been searching for the key for centuries, I very much doubt that they came up with the scheme to exile all dragon-shifters to your world after their spy saw us together in the forest," Taron soothed. "Besides, ridding Elysia of us may be their ultimate goal, but one try to obtain the key may be all a majority are prepared to gamble at this time.

"After all, along with the one that died to snatch you, at least two more that I am aware of had already been sacrificed when I was exiled and Cabak was sent to your world to either kill or capture me. Worst of all, to open the portal to exile me required them to use not only the life-force of an extremely powerful *Ansi* but also the entire power contained within the Dragon Fire of one of the royal guards who was in that tower with me that cursed day. Such expensive losses and unforgiveable atrocities done for no return may lose the leaders much if not all support for an endeavor that never had much hope of succeeding in the first place."

"But think about it," Briana insisted. "I have a key that essentially thumbs its nose at the horrible price those *Ansi* and that poor dragon guard paid for what amounted to a costly failure in the end. At least, I've never felt any pain or weakness the two times I've used it. True, they might not try a hundred times or even ten, but I don't see them giving up on snatching me again if the opportunity arises for a magical item that allows them to cast such high-level spells without the terrible consequences."

"The only reason they managed to snatch you back in the forest was that you had been standing in the same fairly visible spot for quite some time," Taron said pointedly. "We won't make that mistake twice. From now on, anytime we're in the open on the ground, I'll just keep you hidden from sight cupped within my hands just as you are now."

Briana squirmed uncomfortably. Taron hadn't had the luxury this time to hold her in the most ideal position, so both arms had gone numb long ago in his tighter-than-usual grip. She cringed to think how they would feel once Taron released her.

"Um, no thanks. My arms already feel like they're about to fall off. I don't think my body can handle being like this much longer without some damage. Seriously, I'm surprised you dragons don't have a better way for a human to travel with you," Briana scolded.

"You are the only human I have or want to soar the skies with," came his prompt answer.

She couldn't help but smile. "That's so cheesy."

"But no less true."

"Can't I just hide behind one of your humongous legs or something?" she pleaded.

"I suppose…" She could hear the frown in his voice.

"Or since we won't be flying, maybe I can just *sit* in your palm, and you can still hide me from sight with your other hand," she quickly amended. The last thing she wanted to do was add unnecessarily to his pile of worries. What was a little more discomfort compared to the agony of possibly watching your brother be brutally killed? "I'll just watch everything through the cracks in your fingers."

"We can do that." He paused and then added, "Everything's going to be okay, Briana. No matter the outcome of this fight for the crown, no *Ansi* will ever touch you again. I swear it."

Briana shivered at the cold determination in his tone. She had already seen him partially destroy a city for her without hesitation. She hoped she would never have to see him do so again.

CHAPTER SEVENTEEN

hen Taron finally landed about five minutes later, perhaps because he was feeling guilty about the discomfort Briana had mentioned, he set her down onto the ground as close to his massive right leg as possible and told her he thought it would be safe for her to stretch her legs for a couple of minutes. He then immediately offered one of his talons for her to carefully slice through the ropes still binding her wrists. She grimaced as she tried to rub out the godawful pins-and-needles sensation in, first, her abused wrists then in her arms now that the blood had started flowing through them properly again.

She saw that they were high up on the edge of a cliff with a clear view of a vast grassland below that Taron informed her was the palace lawns. Higher still to the left along the face of a mountain whose peak lay hidden within the clouds, she could just make out the palace, itself, a magnificent structure carved directly out of the face of that mountain. An army of thousands of fire-drakes waited in formation at the base of the mountain beneath the shadow of the palace.

As Briana looked to the right, her mouth went dry when she saw an equally impressive army of blue stone dragons. She had been worried that saving her had made him late to the one fight he couldn't afford to miss, but it didn't appear as if anything had happened yet, thankfully.

"A front row seat to the fight of the century starring my older brother," Taron growled bitterly. "We should all be so lucky."

She reached over and rubbed over the scales of his leg in a manner that she hoped was soothing. Could he even feel her touching his scales or were they like fingernails? So many questions she hadn't had time to ask him about his nature. She prayed with everything in her that when this was all over, she would get that chance to ask them.

Briana's attention turned back to the scene unfolding far below them. She squinted as she saw one of the stone dragons in the front break off and fly to the center of the field.

"That's the bastard who started all of this," Taron snarled, his rage almost palpable. "Jathar."

Almost immediately, the stone dragon formation split down the middle with military precision, and a lone firedrake flew through the opening from the back. She didn't need to see Taron stiffen to know that the red and black dragon was Dagon.

"Fool," Taron muttered, his pain now more apparent with his voice booming down on her from above.

"Why didn't he wait to challenge Jathar until he had been awake for at least a month, hell even another day?" Briana found herself asking, her eyes riveted to the two dragons squaring off. "I don't understand."

"We are never more invigorated, more powerful than after the Sleep," he answered, sounding more disgusted than happy about such an obvious boon.

"Jathar must know this. Why would he accept with the odds so out of his favor?"

"Long ago, Jathar was once my father's greatest warrior. Perhaps that's why he was not content with his lot. Those of the House of Blue Stone have always prided themselves on their strength, believing that the most powerful beings in all things should rule. Given this philosophy, it's not a surprise that they allied themselves with a non-shifter people strong in magic such as the *Ansi*.

"My family, well, we're more scholarly than warriors, I suppose. Our strength lies in our knowledge, our wisdom. This has always been a point of contention between our two houses, but the various noble houses of the stone dragons have always respected us for that strength—until Jathar. The Houses flocked to his banner without hesitation. We should have known it was really a grudging respect, at best."

"And Dagon?"

"He believes that today is the only day in which he has a good chance of winning, today when both his mind and body are optimized to one hundred percent vitality. He is—right," Taron admitted reluctantly. He then lowered one clawed-hand to the ground in front of her. "Hop on. The fight will begin any moment now."

Briana nodded and climbed somewhat stiffly onto the smooth scales of his palm, settling herself cross-legged in the center. Taron raised his hand and rested the edge against his chest, only then cupping his other hand loosely over her. Even so, there was still plenty of room for her to see everything in the horizontal space between both hands.

A few seconds later, two roars sounded from below as both dragons leaped into the air, and Briana couldn't help clutching at her knees in anxiety. It had begun.

There was no turning back now, and she had never felt more frightened in her life.

The two dragons slammed into each other a split-second after the dragon king unleashed a stream of death-fire right into Jathar's face. However, the other shook it off as though he had only been sprayed in the face with a water gun and immediately went for Dagon's jugular, smoke pouring from his blue face as he managed to only slice a tooth harmlessly across the scales on his king's neck.

"Can he—actually *bite through* Dagon's scales?" Briana asked faintly, horrified that she might actually witness something so gruesome.

She was immensely relieved when she looked up and saw Taron shake his head through the gaps in his fingers, but it was short-lived. "No. A dragon's scales are impenetrable by tooth, claws, or sword. The trick is to use them effectively as a distraction while hitting the few points of vulnerability we do have—eyes, ears, an open mouth, and most importantly, our necks. They may be covered in scales, but they can still be crushed in the powerful jaws of a dragon if bitten just so."

Suddenly, Dagon's wings folded back onto his back as he latched onto the stone dragon with his talons on both hands and feet, and he started to drop like a rock, taking a startled Jathar with him into the beginnings of a death spiral. She both heard and felt Taron gasp as Dagon did some weird-looking upward flip of his hind legs, the result making Jathar's fall even more unstable as the stone dragon's flapping wings struggled to right himself with Dagon still awkwardly clinging to a space just above both wing joints with the talons on his hands.

Seconds away from crashing into the ground, Dagon abruptly released Jathar and unfurled his wings, having time for only one mighty flap upwards with all his might before he turned sharply to the side and hit the ground rolling. Even though Jathar had been flapping his wings like mad the entire time, due to Dagon's strange acrobatics, his wings never got any lift, and he slammed brutally into the ground.

"Looks as though Dagon found one more point of vulnerability," Taron said in something like disbelief. "If Jathar didn't just break every bone in his body, then I'll eat my own tail. Even a dragon's scales can't protect us against an impact from that kind of fall…"

The stone dragon lay still and silent where he had fallen in the center of a small crater of his own making, one of his wings bent at an odd angle and crushed beneath the bulk of his body. From so high up, she couldn't tell if he was dead or just unconscious.

"Dagon hit the ground pretty hard, too," Briana said worriedly as she watched the dragon king continue to tumble uncontrollably across the palace lawns in a whirl of reds and blacks.

Taron's fingers quivered and flexed slightly, betraying his desire to rush to his brother's side. To be unable to help a loved one in obvious need was pure torture, even for her who barely knew Dagon.

After what felt like an eternity holding her breath, Dagon finally stopped rolling and fell still for another heart-stopping eternity. What if he, like Jathar, was too injured to get up? In a fight to the death, was there such a thing as a draw if neither one could even get up to finish the other?

Then a rush of adrenaline surged through her as Briana saw Dagon lift his head and shake it vigorously before staggering up onto all four limbs.

"You foolish, crazy bastard!" Taron growled, the anger in his voice belying the blatant relief in those large eyes.

Briana scooted on her knees closer to the opening between Taron's hands in her excitement as she watched the dragon king flap his wings once and then walk stiffly over to the rim of the crater Jathar's impact had punched into the lawn. He peered down for a brief moment at his fallen opponent before suddenly turning towards the silent army of stone dragons at his back and shouting several phrases in the Draknar language that seemed to reverberate to the four corners of the world and send ripples of unrest throughout the enemy ranks.

"What did he say?" Briana demanded.

Taron's tone was gleeful as he translated, " 'Let this serve as my judgment for the murder of my father, the late King Lyven of the House of the Red Flame.' "

Then without further preamble, Dagon jumped down into the crater. He picked up Jathar's limp head and pried open his mouth. Like watching a train wreck, Briana couldn't turn her gaze away even though she could guess what was coming.

Dagon opened his mouth, and a burst of orange-red flames flowed from his mouth into the mouth of his enemy for at least a full minute. When Jathar's smoking body hit the ground again, this time, Briana had no doubts that he was dead.

The battle was won, and now the hardest part of the war would truly begin—the aftermath.

EPILOGUE

"Why am I not surprised to find you out here instead of where I left you?" Taron said with a chuckle as he stepped up behind her and slid his arms around her waist.

"Your suite was a bit too gloomy for my current mood," Briana replied, turning around in his arms so that she could look up at his face.

She was dressed in a multi-layered, robe-like dress in white and gold that Taron informed her was worn by the nobility for celebrations. It was both comfortable and beautiful, two things that were not usually mutually true when it came to formal dresses. When she had first seen it, she had been immensely relieved that no corsets were involved.

With the dress and standing out on the extensive

balcony outside Taron's living room that was large enough to hold at least three dragons, looking out from the side of a high mountain with several dragons flying overhead as the sun had begun to set, Briana had felt as though she had entered the pages of a fairytale. The faint outline of a very familiar skyline in the distance just made everything she had seen seem even more surreal. No matter how she had looked at it, that was the freaking Dallas skyline, the result of a natural thinning of the barrier between the two worlds according to Taron, and one more shock to round out such a traumatic day.

The sight of it both intrigued and freaked her out.

See but unable to touch. At least on this end. None of Elysia could be seen on earth—at least not yet. Taron had speculated that it was because of the time discrepancies between the two worlds, that in another hundred or so years, people on earth would likely start seeing faint images of an alien world just as Taron's people had. Using that logic, how long would it be before whatever separated the two worlds thinned enough that they started to physically affect each other?

"Considering that no one has lived in these rooms for about three centuries, I'm not surprised that it feels a bit stuffy," Taron agreed, bringing Briana out of her uncomfortable musings. "A little airing out should fix that particular problem within a month or two."

"That's assuming I'll be here long enough to enjoy the end results."

He instantly went rigid. "You are still unsure about staying? Unsure about *me*?"

Briana pulled out the dragon key from where it hung on a new chain of gold under the collar of her dress. Might as well address the enormous elephant in the room now while they were still alone.

Taron recoiled from it as though it were a cobra.

"Honestly? I just don't know." She took a deep breath and forced herself to continue, "The part about you, about us? Surprisingly, that's the easy part. I've only known you for a couple of days, but it already feels like we've known each other for a lifetime. Now, I just have to decide if I can bear giving up all of the people I care about in my world forever for a life here in this world, a world I hardly know at all. A world where a bunch of fanatical witches want to force me to screw over both your people and mine. I'm not sure if I can ever make that decision."

"Then don't make it tonight," Taron said firmly. "Leave all your worries about the *Ansi* and your safety, the dragon key's safety, from their machinations completely to the royal guards and me. They are currently confined to their city under round-the-clock guard for the foreseeable future. Let me show you the joy of my people, the beauty of my kingdom. What better way to start than a celebration of victory? A celebration of a kingdom starting on a path of healing?"

Briana looked down at the key resting in her palm. If, in the end, she decided that she couldn't bear to leave her homeworld behind, the longer she stayed here and the more time she spent with Taron would make leaving him hurt that much more. She looked back into Taron's earnest eyes. She didn't want to hurt him, but she would be doing just that, even if she left tonight.

Suddenly, the weight of the key in her hand disappeared. Startled, her attention instantly shot back down to her palm, but only the gold chain remained. She stared at it for another few seconds, her brain unable to comprehend what she was seeing.

"The dragon key—disappeared…"

Hearing the bewilderment in her own voice gave Briana an absurd urge to giggle.

"What?" Taron asked sharply, looking down at the hand that now only held a chain with a look as though he thought she was yanking *his* chain.

"Well—Granny Ruth was always nagging me about going out into the world in search of adventure rather than spending my days hovered over an old tome,"

Briana said slowly, the beginnings of a smile forming on her lips as she released the necklace and let her hand drop back down to her side. "It seems the universe agrees."

When the implications of what she said finally sank in, Taron gathered her more tightly into his arms and spent the next few minutes kissing her senseless. "I promise we'll have great fun together, Absorption Girl," he said once he allowed her to breathe again.

She laughed. "No doubt. Royals are always a magnet for trouble, remember?"

"That's why you will be needing this."

A burst of incredible heat suddenly stabbed into her chest, making Briana cry out and clutch hard at the back of Taron's tunic. It was immediately followed by the most enormous surge of adrenaline through her entire body that she had ever experienced, making her feel as though she could suddenly *fly*.

Her pulse racing, Briana squirmed within his arms, the urge to do something, *anything*, was suddenly almost overwhelming. She had never felt so *alive*! She wanted to run through the forest again with Taron, to dance, to make love, to soar the skies. Then in the next breath, that strange euphoria abruptly disappeared, leaving only dizziness and a sense of confusion in its wake.

"What—did you just *do* to me?" she panted, looking up at him with wide eyes.

Taron planted a teasing kiss on the end of her nose. "You didn't think the length of a human life with you would be enough, did you? I just merely gifted you with a portion of my Dragon Fire to ensure we will have centuries of fun together."

The look on his face was smug.

"*Merely?*" Briana echoed a bit shrilly. "You just essentially granted me immortality like a damned genie handing out wishes, and you act as though it's no big deal! What if you just cut your own lifespan short by doing that, you big, reckless lizard! Or—"

Briana yelped as she suddenly found herself tumbled onto her back with a darkening sky overhead and a wickedly-grinning dragon-shifter prince between her legs looking down at her with eyes of flame.

"Perhaps I need to reenact our activities from last night to teach you the meaning of the word 'fun,' " Taron growled.

A burst of heat rose to her face even as her sex began to throb in sudden arousal. Briana raised her hands to cradle his face lovingly. She had a sneaking suspicion that he would win a lot of future arguments this way.

She could always worry about eternity and the ghostly Dallas skyline in the distance tomorrow.

Briana wrapped her legs snugly around Taron's waist and thrust her hips up to rub teasingly against his hardness. "Then teach me, for the rest of our lives."

Needless to say, they were super late to Dagon's victory banquet. In the years to come, it would become a regular occurrence.

WHEN FIRE DRAGONS FALL

DRAGON SHIFTERS OF ELYSIA BOOK TWO

It's raining men...sort of.

After waking up to a severe snowstorm, schoolteacher
Emma Miller thinks the most exciting things she would
do while snowed in at home are stream a few movies
and sip hot chocolate. However, when a breaking news
report of a sizeable island with unnatural structures
suddenly appearing off the coast of England throws a
wrench into her plans, she never dreams that shocking
incident across the pond would repeat in Texas until a
scorching hot—in more ways than one—dragon shifter
crashes into her back yard, putting him at her mercy at a
time when sheltering him could get her arrested.

Dragon shifter Sevek was warned over and over by the
royal scholars not to fly too close to the ghostly city of
another world that was currently bleeding into Elysia.
Ignoring their warnings during one of his patrols, he
consequently finds himself severely injured and trapped
within the very alien world he has been obsessing over
for centuries, forced to rely on Emma, a Terran woman
whose sweet scent awakens desires he hasn't felt in

years. Princess Briana warned his people about the danger her home world's governments would pose should they discover the existence of dragons, a danger he sees with his own eyes. It would be stupid to court a woman who could betray him to her leaders at any moment no matter how much Emma's lovely blushes suggest she would be receptive to his advances. His priority should be getting home without exposing his dragon nature, not chasing after a potential mate he may not get to keep...

Two worlds collide in this thrilling and steamy paranormal romance adventure!

NOW AVAILABLE!

ABOUT THE AUTHOR

Cristina Rayne is a *New York Times* and *USA Today* best-selling author who lives in West Texas with her crazy cat and about a dozen bookcases full of fantasy worlds and steamy romances. She has a degree in Computer Science which totally qualifies her to write romances. As Fantasy is her first love, she feels if she can inject a little love into the fantastical, along with a few steamy scenes, then all the better. She is the author of the *Elven King*, *The Elven Realms*, *Riverford Shifters*, *Dragon Shifters of Elysia*, *Incarnations of Myth*, *The Vampire Underground* paranormal romance series, and the *Fractured Multiverse* science-fantasy series.

www.cristinarayneauthor.com

facebook.com/CristinaRayneAuthor
twitter.com/CRayneAuthor
amazon.com/author/cristinarayne
goodreads.com/Cristina_Rayne